"Put me down, Nick!" she said crossly

Her heart was beating wildly at being held in his arms.

"This path can be rough. I don't want those pretty feet hurt." He was openly teasing her, amused by her discomfort.

"If you don't put me down, one of your pretty blue eyes will get blackened," she said furiously, horrified at her strong reaction to being cradled against his cheek.

"Try it and see what happens." Nick's reply was mocking. "I've had more unarmed combat experience than you. Not that I'd dream of hurting you. There are better ways of subduing an aggressive woman . . . if she's as attractive as you."

His gaze shifted to her mouth. "The last time you were in my arms, you seemed to like it."

Anne Weale and her husband live in a Spanish villa high above the Mediterranean. An active woman, Anne enjoys swimming, interior decorating and antique hunting. But most of all, she loves traveling. Researching new romantic backgrounds, she has explored New England, Florida, Canada, Australia, Italy, the Caribbean and the Pacific.

PINK CHAMPAGNE
Anne Weale

Harlequin Books

TORONTO • NEW YORK • LONDON
AMSTERDAM • PARIS • SYDNEY • HAMBURG
STOCKHOLM • ATHENS • TOKYO • MILAN
MADRID • WARSAW • BUDAPEST • AUCKLAND

Original hardcover edition published in 1991
by Mills & Boon Limited

ISBN 0-373-03216-1

Harlequin Romance first edition August 1992

PINK CHAMPAGNE

CHAPTER ONE

FRIDAY was one of those days. Rosie's lunch was a sandwich at her desk. She had already cancelled her dinner date and left a message on her home answering machine that she would be in for supper but late—she wasn't sure how late.

In fact it was after nine when she flopped, tired but with the satisfaction of having left nothing undone, into the back of the taxi she had called to take her from her office in central London, near Covent Garden, to the house in Fulham she shared with Sasha Otley, another determined career girl, and Clare Bardwell, the older woman on whom they depended for all their creature comforts.

It was several years since Rosie had had to travel to and from work by bus or tube. But having an elastic expense account hadn't made her blasé. When she saw tired faces at bus stops she was conscious of her own good fortune.

The fact that hard work had had a lot to do with it did not diminish her feeling that she was exceptionally lucky. She enjoyed her job and the long hours it involved. Even a day like today, fraught with every possible snag which could disrupt the smooth running of one of London's most successful public relations agencies, was in its way more fun than an easy day in most people's working lives.

As for having to call off her date, that was no great disappointment. Carl was a useful contact and a pleasant man who, if she had been agreeable, would have liked to end their evenings together in bed.

But that, as she had made clear from the outset, was not on. So they saw each other about once a month and talked shop—he was in advertising—and that was as far as it went...as far as any of her relationships with men went.

Rosie was twenty-seven and, at an earlier stage of her life, had tried very hard to fall in love. But after a couple of unsatisfactory relationships she had given up hoping to meet the love of her life and concentrated on her career.

Now she hardly gave love a thought, firmly sublimating her biological urges when they arose, which wasn't all that often. Sometimes she wondered if she was under-sexed. Only one man had ever made her ache with longing to share his bed.

But, as her mother's daily help was in the habit of saying, 'You can't have everything in this life,' and already, Rosie knew, she had more than most women. An absorbing and well-paid job. A happy family background in Yorkshire, and a comfortable home here in London with, in effect, the services of a housekeeper, cook and lady's maid. Holidays abroad. Designer clothes. Lots of friends and plenty of social life.

The only thing lacking was a man to love, to be loved by. But having once experienced the misery of unrequited love, and from all she had seen of other women's love lives, it seemed that men were often more trouble than they were worth. Maybe she was better off without one.

Half an hour later, up to her armpits in the warm, swirling, scented currents of the jacuzzi bath she and

Sasha had installed last year, with a tall glass of gin, ice, lemon peel and slimmers' tonic within reach of her hand, she flipped through the pages of a weekly publishing trade magazine she hadn't had time to look at during the day.

A few minutes later, skimming one of the columns, she was jolted out of her luxurious relaxation by a name she had never expected to see in that context.

A name she would have liked to forget except that, from time to time, she heard it announced on the news on television and always made a point of not watching the item which followed.

Although recently publishers have become more cautious about paying massive advances for potential bestsellers, it took a high six-figure bid from Bury & Poole to win the auction for Nick Winchester's first thriller.

Like Frederick Forsyth, Winchester started his career as a newspaperman before turning to TV, where he is well known to viewers for his reports from the world's trouble spots. Now, as Forsyth did, Winchester has turned his talents to fiction and it's said that his first attempt could even outsell Forsyth's current bestseller.

'It's brilliant: tautly written and packed with action and suspense. Also the sex scenes—often a weak point in books by and for men—are brilliant. I couldn't put it down,' enthuses Carolyn Campden, B & P's fiction director.

Normally, Rosie's first reaction on reading an item of this sort would have been to wonder who would get the job of promoting the book. Her own was one of several agencies which specialised in 'hyping' books for publishers and there was a good chance that Bury & Poole's publicity director, for whom she had organised several successful promotions, would choose her to handle this one.

But in spite of the prestige and money involved, did she want to handle the promo for a book by a man who had once caused her so much heartache?

Nick Winchester had been, and no doubt still was, a man who attracted women easily, and who took full advantage of his opportunities for conquest.

Without even trying, he had swept Rosie off her feet. Not difficult when he had been an experienced twenty-five and she an ingenuous seventeen.

For four months she had lived in a fool's paradise, convinced that her feelings about him must eventually be reciprocated. Then he had walked out of her life, leaving her to face the painful truth that she had meant nothing to him.

Dropping the magazine on to the bath mat spread in readiness for her by Clare, who had also filled the tub while Rosie was undressing and taking off her make-up, she reached for her drink.

Ten years ago, when she and Nick had been working on the same newspaper, she as a trainee journalist and he as the best reporter on one of the most admired provincial morning papers in Britain, she had drunk only fruit juice. Ten years was a long time, especially the years between seventeen and twenty-seven. In ten years' time probably she wouldn't look or be much different from her present self. But a decade ago she hadn't begun to get her act together.

Presently, rising from the water and reaching for the thick white towel Clare had hung over the heated rails at one end of the bath, Rosie looked with satisfaction at the steam-misted reflection of her small-waisted, slender figure in the mirror on the opposite wall.

At seventeen, overfed by a mother who had given up the battle with her own weight and delighted in baking cakes and serving fattening sweets, Rosie had been far too plump. It was only when she left home to live in a bed-sit that she had begun to slim down and to improve her appearance in other ways.

Mum was a dear, in some ways an ideal parent. But it had to be said that she knew nothing about dieting and less about clothes. On the other hand she was unfailingly sympathetic and helpful when anyone was in trouble and Rosie knew that her own ability to get on the same wavelength as almost everyone she met, from a bishop to a bag-lady, was a gift inherited from Mrs Middleton.

As she finished drying her ears, neck and shoulders, she pulled off the shower cap which had kept her hair out of the way. It fell into a silky bell several shades lighter and infinitely more sophisticated than the mid-brown over-permed mop she had had in her first job.

Fortunately most of the things she couldn't change—her basic bone-structure, her eyes, her mouth—were not bad. Transforming herself from the naïve teenage lump Nick had known had been largely a matter of making the best of her natural assets. Even her eyes, always her best feature, looked larger now her face was thinner, and a more striking grey since she had learnt to use liner and shadow with greater subtlety.

The telephone rang. Wrapping the towel round her, Rosie stepped out of the tub and picked up the receiver.

'Hello.'

'Rosie? Hi! How are you?' The publicity director of Bury & Poole had a distinctive voice which made it unnecessary for her to announce her identity to people who knew her as well as Rosie did.

'I'm fine, Anna. How are things with you?'

'All go as usual. Have you heard about our latest coup?'

'You mean the Winchester book?'

'I do indeed. Everyone's over the moon about it. You should be too. We want you to handle his tour.'

'That's a great compliment, Anna, but I'm not sure I'll be free. I've a lot of commitments lined up.'

'Oh, come on, don't play hard to get. You'd give your eye-teeth to do it. Never mind that the book can't fail to bestsell, the man is a dish and what's more he's unattached. No ex-wife, no permanent girl-friend...but definitely no boyfriends. He's the answer to a maiden's prayer.' A contralto chuckle. 'If I weren't a faithful wife, I'd take him on tour myself.'

'Have you actually met him, Anna?'

'Not yet, but I've seen him on TV, exuding char-isma in situations which would have me sweating with terror and screaming, "Get me out of here!" Don't tell me he doesn't switch you on. I shan't believe you.'

'It's a long time since I last saw him. I don't often watch the news on TV. I pick it up on the radio late at night or in the morning. Most of my viewing is videos of the breakfast and prime-time chat shows. That way I can whizz through the parts I don't want to see and just watch the interviews we've lined up...or our competitors have lined up.'

'I do that too, but John likes to catch the news——' Anna's husband was a political agent '—and although one gets sick of seeing the same old catalogue of wars and disaster night after night, year after year, I always perk up and pay attention when Nick Winchester comes on. I think I should quite enjoy being stuck in a tight spot with him, and I bet a lot of other women feel the same way. Let's have lunch early next week? I'd like to talk through our marketing strategy with you. How about Tuesday?'

At Clare's suggestion, Rosie had her supper of smoked salmon with scrambled eggs and a small green salad on a tray in bed. When she had finished eating she looked through *Hello!* to see if this week's issue of the magazine included Sasha's photos of and article about a well-known actress.

While Rosie was training to be a reporter, Sasha had been a trainee photographer on the same paper, with the advantage that her father was chief photographer on another provincial newspaper so she had already learnt a lot from him.

The two girls had often worked together and had remained close friends after Rosie had decided to change to PR work and Sasha had given up staff work to turn freelance.

When the telephone rang again, it was Sasha on the line, calling from Scotland where she had been taking pictures for a brochure about a new country house hotel.

'It's been a tough week. I'm having an early night to iron out the bags under my eyes for our party tomorrow. I suppose Clare's got everything organised with her usual efficiency,' was Sasha's opening remark.

'I should think so. I haven't asked yet. I was late home tonight and we haven't had much conversation. Why have you had a tough week?'

'The weather has made it difficult to get good outdoor shots and also the chairman of the company is a bottom-patter,' said Sasha. 'The sort who ignores a polite brush-off. This afternoon he got really over-heated. I suppose I ought to be used to fighting my way out of unwelcome hugs and treat them as an oc-cupational hazard. But it always makes my blood boil, a middle-aged Casanova assuming, without a shred of encouragement, that I can't and won't resist him. Oh, well, *c'est la vie*. How was your week?'

'Not bad . . . until about thirty minutes ago. Then Anna rang up and dumped a dilemma in my lap. She wants me to handle the promo of a book they've just bought for a lot of money.'

'Where's the dilemma in that?' asked Sasha.

'The book is by Nick Winchester.'

There was a pause before Sasha said, 'Hm . . . yes, I see. But that was long ago and far away. You're not the simple soul you were in those days, Rosie. Surely you can't still have a weak spot for him?'

'No, no . . . of course I haven't,' Rosie said quickly. 'But I'd rather not meet him again . . . be reminded how stupid I was.'

'Not stupid at all. If I hadn't been in love with Tom at that time, I'd probably have fallen for Nick myself. What sort of book has he written? Part one of his autobiography?'

'No, it's fiction...a thriller. Don't know much about it yet. Sounds like what's known in the trade as an airport novel. Something to take the travelling executive's mind off his troubles en route to a conference in Tokyo or LA.'

'When is it coming out?'

'Don't know that either. But I'm lunching with Anna on Tuesday...which doesn't give me long to think up a convincing reason why I can't take it on.'

'Don't be crazy: you must take it on. Big-budget stuff means a fat rake-off for you. Apart from the money, think of the kudos. You'd be mad to turn it down, Rosie. Anna would be narked...and with reason. I know you're good at your job, but so are your rivals. If you put Anna's back up, she might never throw another plum in your direction.'

'I could tell her the truth,' said Rosie.

'The truth wouldn't make any sense to her. You had a teenage crush on a man a long time ago, so you're scared of meeting him again. What does that make you sound like? An idiot, that's what.'

'I suppose it does rather,' Rosie conceded. 'But the fact is I'm scared, Sasha. No, not *scared*. That's too strong a word. Apprehensive is nearer the mark. Falling for Nick, as I did, was the first bad thing that ever happened to me...the worst experience I've had. Isn't it natural not to want to revive all that foolish anguish?'

'Why should working with him revive it? You're not a starry-eyed seventeen-year-old any more. You're an achiever, a success. It doesn't seem to have struck you, but this is an opportunity to turn the tables on Nick.'

'What do you mean?'

'Make him fall for you. Why not? You don't seem to realise what a knockout you are these days. Somehow, in spite of all the evidence to the contrary, somewhere deep down in your subconscious you still keep an out of date image of yourself as you were way back. It's high time you junked it, Rosie. The Rosalind Middleton other people see bears no resemblance to the way you were then. If you really put your mind to it, you could have Nick's scalp on your belt with no trouble at all.'

'How you exaggerate. OK, so I can afford to buy better clothes and my hair looks like hair, not a bird's nest. That doesn't make me irresistible. Anyway I don't want Nick's scalp. I don't want anything to do with him.'

'We'll talk about it tomorrow. I'll be back by mid-afternoon, which will give us plenty of time for a heart-to-heart before the party. Now don't lie awake agonising. Think about where we might go for this year's main holiday. See you tomorrow. Bye.'

Not long after Sasha had rung off there was a tap on the door and Clare came into the bedroom.

While Rosie was having a bath, Clare had taken away the suit and shoes her co-employer had worn that day and now was bringing them back, the suit pressed and spot-checked, the shoes polished and stuffed with tissue paper. It was likely that Rosie's underwear and tights had already been rinsed out and her silk shirt carefully hand-washed and rolled in a towel.

'Clare, I've told you before about working overtime. Those could have waited till tomorrow.

You're supposed to relax in the evenings,' she remonstrated.

Their housekeeper flashed a smile at her before hanging the suit in the wardrobe. 'There's nothing worth watching on TV and I've finished the sweater for Angie. Tomorrow I'll have Sasha's clothes to sort out. Is there anything else I can get you?'

'No, thanks. That was delicious. How was your day?'

'Much less pressured than yours. I spent the morning cooking for the party and this afternoon I went to the new exhibition at the Tate Gallery. A very nice day,' said Clare.

Wondering if the older woman really was as contented as she appeared to be, Rosie asked some questions about the exhibition before saying, 'Sasha rang a few minutes ago. She expects to be back around three. I hope you know how much the way you look after us is appreciated, Clare. We never stop thanking our lucky stars that you answered that advertisement in the *Lady*.'

'It was lucky for me that I saw it. There aren't many housekeeping jobs which would suit me as well as working for you two. Would you like breakfast in bed as you don't have to go to the office tomorrow?'

'You'd spoil me rotten if I let you. No, tomorrow I'm getting up early and going for a workout at the club. Then I'll give you a hand with moving the furniture for the party before my hair appointment.'

Clare picked up the supper tray. 'I'll say goodnight, then.'

'Goodnight.'

After the door had closed quietly behind her, Rosie spent a few minutes wondering, as she had many times before, about Angie's father and the reason why he and Clare weren't together.

She had come to them with excellent references, which they had checked, from two employers in the country, both of whom had been loath to lose her when she had wanted to change jobs in order to be near her daughter, now a music student in London.

But although she was unquestionably a treasure, who ran their house as if it were her own home and who was an inspired cook, Rosie and Sasha knew little about Clare's background. They knew she had been orphaned early in life and, having neither husband nor family to help her, had taken to housekeeping as the only way to support herself and her child, born when she was nineteen, the age Angie was now. But those were the only personal details she had confided.

Rosie's theory was that something similar to her own experience with Nick had happened to Clare, but with more disastrous consequences. Although the existence of a lovable, talented girl like Angie could scarcely be counted a disaster.

The two of them occupied the attic floor which had been made into a self-contained flat. On the first floor were Rosie's and Sasha's bedrooms, their shared bathroom and Sasha's darkroom. The ground floor had been opened up into a large living-room; and in the basement was the kitchen, a cloakroom and a small cosy room with a TV in it.

In spite of Sasha's admonition not to lose sleep over Nick, Rosie found it impossible not to think about him while, before turning out the light, she ran a video of the chat show which had been screened while she was still at the office.

If anyone else who was frequently seen on TV had written a book, she would have jumped at the chance of masterminding the promotion. But Nick . . . all her instincts recoiled from being forced into a situation of considerable intimacy with him.

Had the book been less important, she could have planned the tour but delegated the job of nannying the author round the country to one of her assistants. As things were, Anna would expect her to undertake that job herself. Which meant hours sitting shoulder-to-shoulder with him on shuttles, or alone in first-class compartments, or even closeted in the back of a chauffeur-driven car, depending on how extensive and lavish a tour was required.

By comparison with the various hitches she had sorted out during the day, the prospect of meeting Nick again seemed like a major earthquake compared with a few minor tremors.

'What a rotten great spanner in the works . . . just when everything was going so well,' she muttered aloud.

For, as Sasha said, there was no way to duck the situation without jeopardising relations with Anna and Bury & Poole.

After the video, she switched over to a live telecast, wanting to put off the moment which would remind her how often, because of Nick, she had cried herself to sleep.

Tonight, when she switched off the light and snuggled under the duvet, she tried very hard to follow Sasha's suggestion and think of exotic locations for their next holiday.

But a mental run-through of the world's most glamorous resorts, some of which they had already visited on shared vacations, was repeatedly disturbed by the vision in her mind's eye of a lean, square-jawed face already, at twenty-five, showing incipient laughter-lines.

'Mirrors in a room, water in a landscape, eyes in a face—those are what give character.'

Rosie couldn't recall the source of the quotation except that it was American, but she could remember clearly the colour of Nick's eyes. Dark blue, like lapis lazuli.

Her parents had a vase made of lapis lazuli ware, the name given to a special type of Wedgwood pottery, deep blue veined with gold.

There had been no gold flecks in Nick's vivid irises, only glints of amusement and, nearly always, the suspicion of a smile lurking at the corner of his well-cut, humorous mouth. How many times, surreptitiously, had she gazed at his mouth, too young and naïve to recognise that it was the mouth of a sensualist with a lusty appetite for women?

He had neither smoked nor drunk too much beer, the common vices among journalists. In an office where most of the men had nicotine-stained index fingers and beer bellies, Nick had been the exception, his long fingers as immaculately scrubbed as a surgeon's and his midriff as flat as an athlete's.

Was he still like that? she wondered. Or had the tough, footloose life of an on-the-spot reporter, no sooner back from one trouble spot than despatched to another, turned him into a hard liquor drinker with a mesh of thread-fine red veins beginning to form round irises which might no longer be as vividly blue as her memory of them?

She found herself torn between a deep reluctance to see the Nick she had known showing the first signs of going to seed, and a hope that he was no longer the charmer he had been.

For it hadn't been only her own heart he had won. In different ways, every woman connected with the paper had succumbed to him, from the chairman of the board's huge-bosomed, formidable wife to the switchboard girls and the cleaners.

With one exception, he had been equally popular with his male colleagues. The only one who hadn't liked him had been a sub-editor with whose wife Nick had had an affair. But Rosie hadn't heard about that until after Nick had left the paper. It had been the final twist of the knife in her heart to discover her idol had been capable of cuckolding someone he worked with.

It wasn't surprising his book contained graphic sex scenes. No doubt they were based on his own extensive experience.

CHAPTER TWO

ANNA was already sitting in one of the comfortable armchairs in the bar of the Groucho Club when, the following Tuesday, Rosie arrived to have lunch with her.

The club, in the heart of Soho, had been established in 1985 as a meeting place for publishers, literary agents and others connected with the book world. Beyond the bar was a small dining-room with, upstairs, another restaurant and a room for private functions.

Rosie was a member of the club, as well as of another West End club, and frequented both regularly. She would have been looking forward to hearing Anna's plans for the new star on Bury & Poole's list if he had been anyone but Nick.

'That was a great party you and Sasha gave on Saturday,' said Anna, as Rosie joined her, after exchanging brief greetings or waves with the other people there whom she knew.

'I'm glad you and John enjoyed it.' As the publicity director beckoned a waiter, Rosie said, 'I'll have the same as you, please.' Anna was drinking mineral water with a twist of lemon in it.

Unlike most male publishers who still conformed to the traditions laid down in the days when publishing had been 'an occupation for gentlemen' and lunch-meetings were occasions for rich meals accompanied by fine wines, the majority of women in publishing—and nowadays there were many in important positions—were inclined to be more abstemious. Salads and seafood, with spring water, black coffee and possibly one glass of white wine was the usual fare when women talked business over the lunch table.

Rosie, who had been trained to notice details and was no less observant now that she had given up journalism, had often noticed that, when the pudding trolley was wheeled to a table occupied by women, usually they waved it away or chose the fresh fruit salad. The rich chocolate gâteaux and *tortes* oozing cream were nowadays a male indulgence.

'Are you free the weekend after next?' Anna asked.

Rosie opened the expensive, neatly organised bag which had long since replaced the cheap, cluttered bags of her youth and took out her engagement diary.

'Saturday or Sunday?' she asked, assuming that she was about to receive an invitation to one of Anna's private parties.

'From late Friday afternoon to mid-afternoon the following Monday.'

Rosie gave her a quizzical look. 'What is this? A Roman orgy?'

'A weekend in Spain. Can you make it?'

'Yes, I can, as it happens. At least I've nothing important on that weekend. But what's it in aid of?'

Rosie knew Bury & Poole had held several sales conferences abroad, taking over a hotel in places like Majorca and Crete to entertain their sales force and tell them about the books they were going to have to sell in the following six months. But their last sales conference had taken place a few weeks ago, so this must be something else.

'Nick Winchester has a house in Spain. He's there at the moment, writing his next book. He doesn't want to upset his working routine by coming to London, so he's suggested that we go to him. Carolyn's spending a week there, or as long as it takes to go through the manuscript of the first book with him. You and I will be there for two days. That should be ample time to go over the marketing strategy and promotion with him. What's more, it should be fun. He lives in some style, I gather. Also the sun will be shining. Which will make a nice change from this weather.'

She leaned over the side of her chair and brought into view a large Jiffy bag. 'This is a copy of the typescript of *Crusade*. You'll want to read it before we meet him. Don't start it in bed if you want to be bright and bushy-tailed the next day. Depending on how fast you read, it'll keep you awake till the small hours or even all night. My light was on until four. Usually, in airport fiction, the love interest is pretty perfunctory and the women are cardboard cut-outs. But this guy knows about women. If he makes love the way he writes it, I envy his girlfriends.'

As she handed over the heavy envelope, a book columnist for a women's magazine came over to speak to her, sparing Rosie the necessity of making a comment while her feelings were still in confusion.

She had expected to have several months in which to brace herself for the *rencontre* with Nick and was taken aback by the prospect of having not only to meet him, but to stay in his house as his guest in less than a fortnight's time.

*   *   *

It was dark when the flight from London reached Alicante, giving Rosie, who had a window seat, a glittering glimpse of the large Spanish port by night as the aircraft swung out over the sea to make its approach to the airport, a little to the south of the city.

Rosie had been to Spain before, but only to Marbella on the Costa del Sol which had been too over-developed and touristy for her taste. She was curious to see what this part of Spain, the Costa Blanca, was like. From what she had heard about Benidorm, its principal resort, it sounded as if it might be much the same if not worse than the Costa del Sol. Yet it must have something to recommend it if Nick, a man who had travelled all over the world and presumably could live where he pleased, had chosen to live here.

Nick. The thought that very soon she would be shaking hands with him made her insides churn with nervousness. Would he remember her? She doubted it.

She and Anna had brought only weekend cases small enough to be stowed in the cabin. But Carolyn Campden had brought two large suitcases. Even for travelling she was wearing a smart suit and high heels. Rosie had the impression that Carolyn had more than an editorial interest in Nick.

The aeroplane landed on time and arrival formalities were brief. Had they not had to wait for Carolyn's luggage to be unloaded, they could have been in a taxi within minutes of stepping on to Spanish soil in a temperature noticeably warmer than the chilly evening in London.

As Anna spoke quite good Spanish, she took charge, telling the taxi driver where they wanted to go and instructing him to take the *autopista*, Nick having told her this would reduce the last lap of their journey to about half an hour.

None of them had eaten the meal provided by the airline. Their host kept Spanish hours and dinner at El Monasterio—once a village monastery—was never served before nine-thirty. Nick had not put himself to the trouble of coming to meet them, but he was expecting them to dine with him.

Up to this point Rosie and Carolyn had not had a great deal of conversation. The fiction director had spent the flight working on a manuscript only half as thick as the bulky MS of *Crusade*. But now, while Anna sat in front chatting to the driver, Carolyn turned to Rosie and asked, 'What do you think of Nick's book?'

'I'm not much of a judge because I don't read many thrillers. In fact hardly any. I thought it was very good.'

'I should try to sound more enthusiastic when he asks your opinion of it,' the other woman advised her. 'Authors are sensitive about their work. Their books are like children to them. Also Nick's contract gives him a good deal more say in its handling than is normal. If he feels you're not totally behind it, he could ask for you to be replaced.'

Rosie knew she ought to reply that she was fizzing with enthusiasm for the project, but it would have been a lie and, although a flair for hyperbole was an essential qualification for her job, she had never been comfortable with blatant untruths or gross exaggerations.

Avoiding an answer, she said, 'But you haven't met him yet, have you? You can't be sure what he's like.'

'I haven't actually met him, no. But we've had long talks on the phone. He started his second book while the first one was being read by the publishers on his short list. He doesn't want to leave Spain until he's completed the first draft. He's a very disciplined man. He starts work at seven sharp, breaks at nine for breakfast and a swim in his pool, and then carries on till lunch at three o'clock. He won't change that routine for us. We shall have to adapt to his regime.'

'It sounds as if he's already rather big-headed. If the book does put him among the top names of that genre, he could become intolerable,' said Rosie.

In the glow from the headlamps of a car they had just overtaken, Carolyn gave her a sharp look. 'He knows his own worth. There's nothing wrong with that. Even if the book had less merit, it would sell because his face is well-known on TV. That, combined with the fact that it's one of the most gripping novels I've read in the last ten years, makes it a sure-fire winner. I'm delighted to have the chance to edit a major new talent.'

'Well, as you have the reputation of being one of the best editors in the business, I think he should feel lucky too,' Rosie said diplomatically. 'How did you start your career?'

Like most people, Carolyn was not unwilling to talk about herself and Rosie listened attentively, partly because she had always been interested in other people's lives and partly as a distraction from the imminent ordeal of meeting Nick.

The taxi was travelling fast and soon the driver was pointing out the clustered high-rise hotels and apartments of Benidorm some distance away on the seaward side of the motorway.

But the little village of Font Vella, which Anna said must take its name from an old fountain or spring, lay somewhere in the dark mountainous hinterland behind the bright lights of the coast.

At last, after leaving the motorway and twisting and turning up a road with a bumpy surface, they saw the name of the village on a sign on the verge and soon after passed a small shop, still open for business, and a bar where several old men could be seen watching TV.

The streets in the centre of the village were so narrow and winding that it was only just possible for the taxi to negotiate them. Children playing by the light of the street-lamps attached to the upper storeys of the houses drew back against the white-washed walls or stepped into doorways to let them pass.

The driver braked to ask one of them the way. Following the boy's directions, he turned a tight corner into a street like a canyon where people on opposite balconies would almost be able to shake hands, and presently emerged into an unexpectedly spacious *plaza* with a church on one side and what was evidently the monastery at right angles to it.

At first sight El Monasterio was not an attractive building. Only a few small barred windows broke the gaunt stone façade, none of them lighted. The massive iron-studded door, near which the driver pulled up, looked as if it had been designed to keep people out rather than encourage them to enter. Indeed the place looked deserted.

As the three women swung their legs out of the taxi and the driver hurried to open the boot and lift out their baggage, Rosie felt a brief spasm of amusement. The possibility that, far from living in style, Nick's life as a roving reporter might have taught him to dispense with all but the most basic necessities appealed to her quirky sense of humour.

Would Carolyn's admiration for him survive the discovery that, having brought a trousseau of smart clothes, she was expected to hang them on nails in the wall of a cell offering little more comfort than its original occupants had enjoyed?

'I'll pay the driver. You ring the bell, Rosie,' said Anna.

Rosie gave an experimental tug on a metal pull and, hearing no sound from within, tugged more vigorously. Whereupon a loud clanging could be heard for above the door was an open transom filled only with a wrought-iron grille, presumably to give light and air to the hall inside. Presently the sound of masculine footsteps on stone flags could be heard.

She held her breath, expecting at any moment to see the face of the man she had once loved.

When the wicket cut in the large door opened, it wasn't Nick who stepped out but a young Spaniard.

'Good evening, ladies,' he said, in English. 'I regret that Señor Veenchester is not here to welcome you himself. He has been called away but should return shortly. But please come inside and Encarna will show you to your rooms.'

At this point Encarna appeared, a dumpy little woman in a pinafore with a friendly smile who greeted them in Spanish.

The interior of the building seemed at first to match the outside. A lofty hall with several closed doors on one side and a stone staircase rising on the other was furnished with a hard bench and heavy oak table and lit by a single dim bulb. There was a marked drop in temperature as if they had entered a crypt or a dungeon.

'Not quite what I expected,' Anna murmured to Rosie, as they mounted the stairs, led by the young man carrying Carolyn's two cases and Encarna carrying theirs.

Rosie gave what was intended to be a philosophical shrug. For her, any physical discomforts which might be in store for them were of little importance compared with her mental unease. She wasn't sure whether to be glad or sorry the confrontation with Nick had been delayed. It seemed very cavalier of him not to be here. What could be more important than being on hand to welcome three guests from London?

The landing at the top of the staircase was as bleak and poorly lit as the hall below. But when the Spaniard opened a door and ushered them through it, they found themselves in the warmer air of a four-sided cloister surrounding a large courtyard, with another cloister beneath it.

And when Encarna opened three doors along the cloister and showed first Carolyn, then Anna and finally Rosie where they were to sleep, their spirits rose. For the rooms allotted to them were neither cramped nor uncomfortable.

Looking around her room and the adjoining bathroom after Encarna had shown her where the light switches were, Rosie wondered about the woman who had helped Nick to furnish the monastery. She couldn't believe he alone was responsible for a bedroom fit for the pages of *House & Garden* or one of the other interior decoration glossies.

However this wasn't the moment to study the décor in detail. She began to unpack the capsule wardrobe she hoped would see her through the weekend.

A tap on the door sent a flutter of alarm through her, in case it was Nick who was out there. Almost instantly she realised that it couldn't be. Even if he had returned, why should he come to her room? Or indeed any of their rooms? He would wait for them to go downstairs.

This is ridiculous. I'm a bundle of nerves over nothing, she thought, as she called, 'Come in.'

It was Anna, bearing the bottle of duty-free gin she had bought on the plane and a bathroom tumbler.

'I could do with another snifter. How about you?'

'A small one.' Rosie had had two gin and tonics in the air. Working in PR had accustomed her to a fairly high alcohol intake but tonight, meeting a new client for the first time—for that was how she must try to think of him—she wanted to have all her wits about her.

'Our first impression was misleading, wasn't it? I began to think I'd be spending the night in a cell but there's nothing monastic about the mattresses and there's plenty of hot water on tap. Every comfort one could wish for,' said Anna. 'I hope dinner isn't too delayed. I'm getting peckish, aren't you?'

Rosie nodded, but in fact nervous tension had destroyed her appetite.

'If Carolyn's finished unpacking, I think we should go down. We might be offered some *tapas* to stave off the worst pangs,' said Anna, when she had swallowed her drink.

Like Rosie, she was still wearing the clothes she had arrived in—black sweater and trousers—but had brushed her hair and retouched her make-up. Anna always wore black with Indian or African jewellery.

Rosie had travelled in immaculate jeans and a cashmere turtle-neck top under a classic hacking jacket. Her accessories were well-polished tassel loafers, a coach-hide bag and a colourful Hermès silk headsquare made in the 1930s and snapped up at a jumble sale during a visit to her parents.

They found that Carolyn had changed into a smart silk frock and dramatic earrings. About the same age as Anna, who was thirty-three, Carolyn had been married but now was divorced.

As she led the way downstairs, they heard a car drawing up outside the monastery. Just as Carolyn reached the hall, the wicket door opened and a very tall man ducked through it.

Seeing them, he said, 'You've arrived! I'm extremely sorry I wasn't here to meet you. Something urgent cropped up which demanded my immediate attention.' He offered his hand to Carolyn. 'You are...?'

'Carolyn Campden. Hello. It's a pleasure to meet at long last.'

'For me also. Welcome to Font Vella, Carolyn.' With practised ease he lifted her hand to his lips.

Although she had seemed self-possessed, the gesture, not common in England, made Carolyn give a small sound of pleased surprise. Then she turned to introduce the others.

'This is Anna Mortlake, our publicity director.'

'As the Spanish say, *mi casa es su casa* ... my house is your house, Anna.'

'Thank you ... it's good to be here.' Perhaps because she was prepared for it, Anna behaved as if having her hand kissed was a commonplace occurrence.

It was she, not Carolyn, who said, 'This is Rosalind Middleton, head of the agency which will be handling your promotion.'

Rosie did not get her hand kissed. He clasped it as if he intended to salute her in that fashion but instead of bending his head he continued to look intently at her. For a moment she thought that in spite of the ten-year interval and the dismal light in the large vestibule he had recognised her.

Then he said, rather formally, 'How do you do? It's good of you to come all this way,' and her hand was shaken and released.

Addressing them all, he went on, 'It's always cold in the hall, except in July and August. Come to the library and get warm. I'm sure you're longing for your dinner. We'll have a quick drink and then we'll eat.'

The library, off the ground-floor cloister, was a huge room with log fires burning in the cavernous hearths at either end. The floor was spread with a vast mat of plaited grass, the same *esparto* as the workman's basket with rope handles which Rosie had bought on her holiday in Marbella. The walls were lined with books; hundreds, perhaps thousands of books, some in old leather bindings, others in shiny new dust-jackets.

At the end of the room a drinks tray shared a large table with more books and magazines. At the other end another table was set for a dinner *à quatre*. There were enough chairs and sofas to seat at least twenty people in relaxed comfort, every seat with a reading lamp and a table for a cup of coffee or a drink close at hand.

'How long have you had this place, Nick?' Carolyn asked, as he went to the well-stocked drinks tray where a bottle of champagne was standing in a bucket of ice.

'Fifteen years. I was twenty when I bought it...one of the many rash acts of my youth.'

His smile had lost none of its charm. In the better light of the library, Rosie saw that his eyes were still vividly blue, if anything bluer than before because now he had the deep tan only possible for someone with almost black hair and olive skin.

'It was going for a song because it was in a bad state and nobody wanted a place of this size with no electricity and the roof falling in,' he went on. 'But I thought it had possibilities. For the first five years I came here every summer and spent what I could afford on putting it to rights. Then I switched from newspaper journalism to TV reporting and began to collect things to put in it. By the time I was ready to try my hand at fiction, it was as you see it now.'

As he spoke, he handed them each a glass of pink champagne. 'All it lacks,' he said, as he picked up his own glass, 'is the proverbial woman's touch and the patter of little feet.'

'You surprise me,' Rosie said coolly. 'I should have said it owed a great deal to a woman's touch... possibly several women's touches.'

She sensed that Carolyn and Anna were surprised, not to say startled by her comment and its tone.

Nick, if he recognised a caustic tone in her remark, said equably, 'It wouldn't look the way it does if I hadn't engaged the services of the man generally re- garded as Spain's most distinguished designer, Jaime Parladé. It was he who brought into harmony all the stuff I'd picked up on my travels. What shall we drink to? How about *salud y pesetas, y tiempo para gozarlas*: health and money and the time to enjoy them.'

As the three women repeated the toast, he raised his glass to each of them in turn before drinking. As before, Rosie was the last to receive his salutation and, as before, he continued to look keenly at her while tasting the sparkling dry wine here called *cava* because, as she had learned on her previous visit, the Spanish growers were forbidden to call it champagne although it was made by exactly the same method as French champagne.

'I think we should also drink to the reason for our being here... your marvellous book,' said Carolyn.

'Quite right. To the book,' Anna agreed with enthusiasm.

'To the book,' echoed Rosie.

'Thank you, ladies. I'm sure any book with you three behind it has an excellent chance of success. Now if you'll excuse me for a moment I'll tell Encarna to serve the meal.'

When he had left the room, Anna said, 'All I can say is wow! He's even more gorgeous in the flesh than I imagined. You never get a proper impression of people's height on TV. I assumed he was tall but he's taller... at least six feet two, wouldn't you think?'

'And all in proportion,' said Carolyn. 'Do you suppose that reference to a woman's touch and the patter of little feet meant he has someone in view? I hope not. I mean, he's far more promotable as an eligible bachelor. Don't you agree?' looking at Rosie.

Rosie couldn't help wondering if Carolyn wanted him to be heart-free for personal rather than professional reasons. There was a definite touch of flirtatiousness in her manner towards him. Perhaps she was like that with all men. Some women were.

'I think in the long run it's the book's appeal, not his, which will sell it,' she answered. 'You can hype a book to the skies but it won't stay in the charts unless it's inherently a winner. Although of course a lot of excellent books never get the sales they deserve for lack of the push to get them started. I think Mr Winchester's charisma and TV exposure must be an enormous help, but the book would make it if he were a recluse.'

Now that the ordeal of meeting Nick was over and he hadn't recognised her, she was less strung up, capable of separating her feelings about him from her feelings about the book.

'As I told Carolyn, I'm not a thriller reader,' she went on. 'But this is more than a thriller. It's a first-class novel which happens to be about the drug war. It should appeal to women as much as to men. I think our efforts are really going to be superfluous. Although it's in a different category, like *Gone With The Wind* and *Rebecca* this book is going to sweep the field, with or without our help.'

'I'm delighted to hear you say so.'

Nick had re-entered the room by another door which, as he closed it behind him, proved to be a clever piece of *trompe-l'œil* with the spines of closely packed volumes so cleverly painted on the wood that at a casual glance no one would guess there was a door among the real bookshelves.

His unexpected reappearance surprised them all, especially Rosie.

'I'm sorry—I didn't mean to startle you,' he apologised. 'I've been to my room to clean up.' He looked at Rosie. 'I'm very glad to hear that you think so highly of the book. As I've had my fill of TV and don't want to go back to journalism, writing is my only option.'

At this point Encarna entered with a tureen of soup and they took their places at the table, Carolyn and Anna on either side of their host and Rosie directly opposite.

'Who is the young man who helped me with my luggage?' Carolyn asked, as she unfolded her napkin.

'José Maria Rodriguez... who's on leave from the Army and likes to practise his English. He was with me when I was called out. As Encarna has no English, I asked him to stand in for me.'

'Is your Spanish fluent?' asked Anna.

'I speak fairly good Castilian Spanish, the lingua franca of the country. But in this part of Spain the people speak Valenciano except when they're talking to foreigners and people from other parts. Now that I'm living here full-time, it shouldn't take long to pick it up.'

'You said something about the patter of little feet. Are a wife and children part of your plan for living here?' Carolyn asked.

'A happy family life is part of most people's plans, isn't it?' he answered. 'Until recently, because of the work I was doing, no woman in her right mind would have taken me on. If *Crusade* sells, I should be a slightly better bet. But so far I haven't met anyone who wants to sequester herself in a monastery in the backwoods of Spain. Are you three married?'

'I am. Carolyn was. Rosie isn't,' said Anna, helping herself to soup. She smiled at Encarna. *'Gracias.'*

As the maid left the room she touched a switch which turned out all but one of the table-lamps and left the round dining table lit by a group of candles and by the light of the fire.

'How did you discover the monastery?' Carolyn asked. 'I shouldn't think many tourists find their way to this village, do they?'

'No, there's nothing here to attract the package tourists, but some of the expatriate community—mostly retired people from the colder parts of Europe and North America—come to the bar in the village to eat the roast leg of lamb which is the speciality of the owner's wife. I found Font Vella when I was staying with a friend whose parents live on the coast. He and I had both been keen on fell-walking and one day we set out to explore the mule paths which criss-cross these mountains. They led us here.'

Rosie was learning things about him she hadn't known before. He must have owned the monastery at the time she knew him, but he had never spoken of it to his colleagues. Nor had she heard him mention fell-walking.

'I have a friend, a photo-journalist, who does a lot of work for *Hello!* magazine,' she said. 'As you know, it's an off-shoot of the Spanish weekly *Hola!* I'm sure both magazines would be interested in a feature about the monastery. Would you have any objection to that? It would be excellent publicity.'

'I must admit that, having once made my living prying into other people's private lives—although never as ruthlessly as the tabloid press do—I'm not particularly keen to have my own life exposed to public view. Is it necessary? Writers like Forsyth and

Deighton don't seem to go in for a lot of personal publicity.'

'They established themselves before publishing became as competitive as it is today,' said Anna. 'I can't urge you strongly enough to agree to anything Rosie suggests.'

'If you like you can write the text of the feature yourself,' said Rosie. 'Sasha won't mind. She's an excellent photographer but not so hot on the written stuff. I usually polish it up for her. She'd be happy to have you collaborate with her.'

Nick was looking fixedly at her but she could tell he wasn't listening to what she was saying.

'My God! Roly-poly Rosie,' he exclaimed suddenly. 'I had a feeling I'd met you somewhere before, but I'd forgotten your surname so Rosalind Middleton didn't ring any bells. It was your eyes I remembered. Everything else about you has changed, but not those beautiful grey eyes.'

Rosie's heart gave a curious lurch, a sensation she had not felt for a very long time; not since the first time he smiled at her. Aware of the others' puzzlement, she felt herself starting to blush.

'For a few months, a long time ago, Nick and I were on the same newspaper,' she said.

'But you must have recognised me. Why didn't you say so?' he asked.

She attempted a nonchalant shrug. 'Does anyone want to be reminded of the way they were at seventeen?'

He laughed, showing the beautiful teeth she remembered from years ago.

'But you were a darling, Rosie. A little on the plump side maybe, but so full of *joie de vivre* and excitement at being taken on as a junior reporter that everybody adored you. I remember Sasha as well. A dark girl with very short hair and large gypsy earrings. She was Tom's girl, I seem to remember.'

'She was then but later they split up,' said Rosie. 'But I'm sure all this reminiscing must be frightfully boring for Anna and Carolyn.'

'You're right. We must get together and talk about old times later. Here comes Encarna with the chicken.'

He rose and collected the soup plates, coming back from the side-table with a bottle of wine to fill the heavy glass goblets which Rosie recognised as coming from Biot in France.

CHAPTER THREE

ROSIE woke at what would have been seven in England and was eight in Spain. It had been long past midnight when they came to bed and Nick had suggested they should get up when they felt like it. He would be busy all morning.

In spite of the very small window overlooking the *plaza*, Rosie's bedroom was not at all gloomy because it had two large skylights let into the restored roof. Watching the pink glow of dawn seeping across the clear sky, she wondered how she could avoid Nick's intended talk about 'old times'.

After dinner, sitting by the fire, Carolyn and Anna had done most of the talking. Rosie had said very little, preferring to let the other two hold the floor while she listened, trying not to notice how the firelight emphasised Nick's handsome bone-structure and turned his deep suntan to bronze. It had crossed her mind that, with his strongly marked features and well-shaped skull, he would be an excellent subject for a sculptor.

If it hadn't been for the fact that he might have insisted on escorting her to her door, she would have retired to bed early. The build-up of nervous tension ever since Anna had told her about this weekend had, once the moment of confrontation was over, left her strangely exhausted.

Soon after eleven there had been a short power-cut which would have plunged them into darkness had it not been for the log fire. Apparently power-cuts were a frequent occurrence in rural Spain, which was why all the visitors' bedrooms were supplied with torches and candlesticks.

The bed in which she was sleeping was one of a pair of wider than average single beds, both with barley-sugar headposts topped with brightly painted carvings of parrots. She guessed that Nick must have picked up one set of posts on his travels and had them copied for the twin bed.

It seemed strange for a man on his own to have acquired goods and chattels. Yet why not? Hadn't she always been a magpie, gradually accumulating pictures, pieces of furniture, rugs and the miscellaneous odds and ends which were now in the house in Fulham? Why shouldn't a man have the same acquisitive instinct?

For the first time it struck her that she had never heard Nick refer to his parents or to any aspect of his past life. He had only talked about the present and the future. Was that because the past was something he preferred to forget?

I was in love with someone I didn't really know, she thought. It was almost like having a crush on a pop singer or a film star. I fell for his eyes, his mouth, his physical presence, but the much more important parts of him—his mind and his heart—I never gave a thought to.

Knowing she wouldn't go back to sleep, and not wanting to lie in bed thinking about Nick, she got up and dressed, putting on soft-soled shoes which would make no sound on the flags of the cloister when she left the room. Both Carolyn and Anna had said they enjoyed getting up late at weekends and she didn't want to disturb them as she passed their rooms.

Last night she had noticed that the cloisters on the far side of the courtyard were open on both sides. But there had been nothing but darkness to be seen beyond the double row of pillars.

This morning the view made her gasp. The monks had built their retreat overlooking a bowl-shaped valley sheltered by mountains to the west and giving a distant prospect of the sea to the east.

Quickly she hurried round to the open side of the cloister, captivated by a panorama as beautiful as any she had seen in her quite extensive travels.

'I used to visualise this when I was in Beirut, and all the other places where children grow up not knowing what a peaceful, verdant countryside looks like,' Nick said quietly.

As it had the night before when he returned to the library by way of the painted jib-door, his soundless approach from the doorway to the upper hall had caught her unawares.

As she swung round, he said, keeping his voice low, 'Good morning. I hope your being up so early doesn't mean you had a poor night.'

'Good morning. No, I slept very well, thank you. I usually get up early. I thought you were always closeted in your workroom at this hour.'

'As a rule, yes. But sometimes I take a short break to come up and look at the mountains. They're at their best in this light. Once the sun gets up, their shapes become less distinct. Also, for writers who use a computer, as I do, it's supposed to be a good thing to have a complete change of focus every so often. After I've been staring at the screen for about an hour,

I rest my eyes by looking at the sierras. Encarna is making coffee. Will you have a cup with me?'

Although a tête-à-tête with him was the last thing she wanted, Rosie felt obliged to say, 'Thank you.'

'We'll have it downstairs on the terrace where our voices won't disturb your colleagues if they're asleep. I see you are sensibly shod,' he said, glancing down at her feet.

He was wearing a pair of navy blue cotton espadrilles with rope soles. Perhaps because his long legs made it difficult for him to find ready-made trousers of the right length, his white denim jeans showed his ankles. They were as brown as his face.

Like Rosie, he was wearing a sweater. Hers was a cream cotton guernsey, a present from her parents after a holiday in the Channel Islands. Nick was wearing a blue naval sweater with cotton elbow-patches and cotton reinforcements on the shoulders. The epaulettes, intended for the wearer's badges of rank, emphasised the breadth of his shoulders which, as Anna had remarked the night before, were in perfect proportion to his height.

Downstairs, he took her to the kitchen where the delicious aroma of freshly ground coffee beans was starting to pervade the air.

Encarna was nowhere to be seen but, as Rosie was looking admiringly at the blue and yellow antique tiles with which the walls of the kitchen were faced up to dado height, the Spanish woman came in by the back door. She was carrying a long cotton bag with 'PAN' embroidered on it.

'The village has an excellent baker,' said Nick, adding something in Spanish which made Encarna open the bag and hand him a long crusty loaf.

Nick broke off the end of the loaf and offered it to Rosie. 'Have the crustiest bit.'

When she had taken it from him, he broke off another piece for himself.

The bread, made with wholemeal flour, was still hot from the oven. But before she could taste it, Encarna shook a reproving finger at Nick and said, *'Momento, señorita...'* with a gesture indicating that Rosie should wait a moment.

She then produced a dish of butter, another of honey, and a plate, knife and checked napkin.

'Encarna can't understand that I find the bread good on its own and she may be right, you may not care for dry bread.' He said something to his housekeeper who nodded and fetched a tray.

By this time Rosie had bitten off a piece of the crust. 'I agree: even by itself it's delicious,' she said.

When Encarna had set the tray with two pottery cups and saucers and a basket lined with another napkin for the bread, Nick picked it up.

'The coffee isn't quite ready. Encarna will bring it to us in a few minutes.'

He led the way along a passage to another door giving on to a covered terrace furnished with basketwork chairs and loungers with faded blue sailcloth squabs and cushions.

The terrace had much the same view as the outer cloisters except that from here more of the monastery garden was visible, including a number of orange trees bearing ripe fruit and, at a lower level, a large swimming pool, its surface at present covered with a thermal blanket. Wisps of vapour seeped up from the edges, indicating that the water was heated.

'How long have you had Encarna looking after you?' Rosie asked, as he put the tray on a cane table and pulled it to where they would be sitting in sunlight.

'Since a year ago when I came to live here permanently. Before that she kept the place aired and looked after the indoor plants and did my laundry in her washing machine when I was here. Sometimes I cooked for myself, sometimes I ate out.'

He fetched a wicker armchair, placed it to face the view, and gestured for her to be seated.

Fetching another for himself, he went on, 'She had been widowed for six months when I packed in TV. She has a daughter married to a chef in Benidorm and they wanted her to sell her house and live with them. But Encarna is a countrywoman. She didn't fancy life in a sixth-floor apartment. So she offered to keep house for me. It's an arrangement which suits us both, but I don't know how long it can last. She doesn't look it, but she's getting on for seventy.'

'I would never have guessed it. She doesn't look much more than sixty. Are those oranges ready to pick?'

'They are. Would you like one for breakfast?' He pushed back his chair and went to fetch one for her, moving with the lithe grace of a man in perfect physical condition.

None of the signs of an unhealthy, dissipated life she had half expected to find were apparent in his muscular physique. The whites of his eyes were as clear as her own.

'Thank you,' she said, when he came back. 'When I was staying in Marbella I bought some tangerines which had leaves on their stalks, but I've never had an orange straight from the tree before.'

'I'll peel it for you...the Spanish way.' He took out a pocket knife and sliced off the top and bottom before making half a dozen longitudinal cuts in the thin glossy peel which then came away very easily.

Watching the swift, precise movements of his lean brown fingers, Rosie remembered a day when he had come past her desk in the *News* when she was new to the job and hadn't completely mastered the software used in that office.

He had realised she was in a muddle, said, 'Move over,' and sorted it out for her, rewriting her report but in a tactful way so that she saw how it should be done but wasn't made to feel a fool. Perhaps it was then, watching his fingers flick expertly over the keyboard and the right words, arranged in the right way, come up on the screen, that she had lost her heart to him.

I mustn't do it again, she thought, as Encarna appeared with the coffee pot in one hand and a jug of hot milk in the other.

'Enough about my life...I want to hear about yours,' he said. 'Where do you live and how did you come to be in charge of a PR agency?'

'I changed to PR six years ago when I didn't get the job I wanted on a women's magazine but was offered one as an assistant to the woman who founded the agency. Two years ago she married an American oil man and I took over the business. I share a house in Fulham with Sasha Otley. Like you, we have a housekeeper to run it so that we can concentrate on our careers.'

'How do you like your coffee? Half and half?' When he had filled both cups Nick gave her a thoughtful look. 'Your parents were farmers, weren't they, Rosie?'

'How clever of you to remember.'

'Not really. I remember you as the archetypal farmer's daughter: a lovely skin, rosy cheeks, rather buxom in those days, a living advertisement for good wholesome food, country air and rural life. I would never have imagined you becoming a sophisticated London career girl. If I'd been asked to predict your future, I'd have said you would stay in journalism for a couple of years and then marry somebody local and settle down to raise a family.'

'You would have been miles off the mark. The last thing I wanted was to be like my mother, stuck in a rut of domesticity. It may not have shown in those days, but I was always ambitious and so was Sasha. Archetypal yuppies, that's what we were...our sights firmly set on being successful careerists.'

'And having, I gather, achieved your objectives, has it made you as happy as you hoped?' he asked.

'Very much so. As you have with this place, in a different form we've achieved a perfect lifestyle.'

'And where do men fit in to this pattern of perfection? Do you have boyfriends?' he asked.

'From time to time, yes, of course. But neither of us plan to become seriously involved for at least another ten years.'

'Is it possible to plan one's serious involvements? Don't they just happen whether the timing is convenient or not?'

'To some people—yes. But I don't think either Sasha or I are likely to lose our heads now. I know I'm not. I like being a woman of independent means. If I'd had a husband and children, I probably shouldn't have been able to fly out here for the weekend to discuss the promotion of your book.'

'Anna is married. She's here.'

'Anna has an exceptionally accommodating husband and no children. The majority of men still aren't keen on their wives flitting about the world and putting their work before their domestic responsibilities. This is delicious honey. Is it local?'

'It's eucalyptus honey from Callosa de Ensarria. Had you been staying longer, I would have taken you there to sample the various flavours and choose some to take back to London. In view of the fact that we're old friends, and you aren't hampered by a husband, can't you extend your visit for a day or two?'

'Unfortunately not. I'm very busy next week, and I'm sure Carolyn is impatient to start going through your book with you. If you're not in a hurry to get back to your desk——' he was spreading honey thickly on a piece of bread '—can we talk business? Do you have any ideas of your own on how the book should be promoted?'

Nick bit off a piece of the bread and chewed it with obvious enjoyment while considering his reply.

'I wouldn't say this if we were strangers. As we aren't, I'll be candid with you. I'm not falling over myself to leave here and trek around the UK helping local radio disc jockeys fill in the time between records. Frankly, I have reservations about the value of these tours, but I don't expect you to agree. They're part of your livelihood. The whole promotional circus was invented by PR people and authors are stuck with it, whether they like it or not. Some of them may enjoy that kind of ego trip. But I'd just as soon stay here, writing and reading.'

His attitude surprised her. She had heard several authors claim that they didn't like promo tours but had never taken them seriously. If they really hated the tours they could refuse to do them, but very few did.

Knowing Anna would be horrified if she heard her, Rosie said, 'In that case, why not do that? Or have Bury & Poole insisted that you help to launch the book in person?'

'No, they haven't made it a condition, but it's what they want and I don't feel I'm in a position to reject their proposals. I'm a greenhorn in the book world and maybe they're right and I'm wrong.' He gave her a glinting blue glance. 'And I must say that now I've met my bear-leader I'm becoming more resigned to the idea. It could turn out to be fun.'

She wondered what he meant by fun. She said briskly, 'I don't think tours are ever that, but we'll do our best to make it as painless as possible. As a journalist yourself you should have no trouble establishing a rapport with the journalists who will interview you. Has Anna given you B & P's author's questionnaire to fill in? Or do you have a curriculum vitae I can use as the basis of a hand-out about you?'

'I have a CV on disk. I'll print out a copy for you later today. Anna mentioned a questionnaire and may have brought it with her. Have some more.' He passed her the basket of bread.

'No, thanks, no more for me. I thought I'd pass the time until the others are up having a look round the village.'

'Why not leave that till later? I'm going to have a swim next. Wouldn't you like to join me? Did you bring a swimsuit? Anna said she would tell you to bring one.'

'Yes, I did and I'd like to swim later but not right now if you don't mind.'

There was a degree of intimacy about having a swim alone with him which she preferred to avoid.

'As you like. How about some more coffee? There's still plenty in the pot.'

Rosie shook her head. 'It was a very good breakfast—especially the orange. I'll see you later.'

As she pushed back her chair and stood up, Nick also rose. He had always been punctiliously courteous to the women on the editorial staff, opening doors for them, lighting their cigarettes, finding bar stools for them to sit on when they joined the men in the pub round the corner.

Other reporters had taken the view that women on equal pay with equal opportunities had no right to expect special courtesies. Perhaps that was one of the reasons for Nick's success with women. He understood that however 'equal' women were, they were still and perhaps always would be suckers for the chivalrous approach.

'It's market day in the village. I shouldn't think you'll see anything you want to buy, but would you like to take a few hundred *pesetas* in case?' he asked, producing a billfold from the back pocket of his trousers. His sudden grin made deep creases down his cheeks. 'A credit card's not much use in Font Vella market.'

'Thanks, but I have some Spanish money.'

Although she was here for only a couple of days, Rosie had thought it wise to bring about fifty pounds' worth of *pesetas*. She might see something her mother would like, or presents for her two sisters, both of whom had done what Nick had predicted for her: married young and had babies.

This morning, when she stepped through the wicket, the *plaza* was full of stalls selling plastic flowers, plastic jewellery, enamel pots and pans, cheap crockery, carpet slippers, track shoes and corsets such as her grandmother had worn except that these were flesh-coloured instead of the shiny pink garments she had seen hanging out to dry on Granny's washing line.

The wares were not dissimilar from those sold on markets in the north of England. The only things she could see which were essentially Spanish were brown glazed earthenware casseroles and rabbit-fur slippers.

But if the market was not exciting, Font Vella, as she wandered around its steep streets and alleys, made her wish she had brought her camera to record the handsome wrought-iron grilles which protected some of the windows, and the heavy brass door-knockers shaped like dolphins or lace-cuffed hands. Where some doors were standing open, she caught glimpses of unexpectedly large and well-to-do interiors.

It was near the entrance to the village that she found the fountain from which the place took its name. Jets of bright water gushed from three spouts and fell into a large stone basin. From there it flowed along a channel at the side of the road and presumably was used to water the cultivated land surrounding Font Vella.

As Rosie was watching the play of sunlight on water, a woman came to fill a plastic container from one of the spouts. The houses must have piped water if Encarna had a washing machine, but perhaps that came from a reservoir in the hills and this was better for drinking.

How civilised, to have natural spring water to drink and good bread from an old-fashioned baker's oven to eat, she thought, strolling back up the steep main street with its time-polished cobbles. In the past, she noticed, the street had been stepped all the way up but now at the sides the shallow steps had been converted into slopes so that cars could drive up and down.

'Good morning, *señorita*.'

She turned to find the young Spaniard who had met them the night before coming up the hill behind her.

'Good morning, Señor Rodriguez.'

'You know my name but I do not know yours,' he said, as they fell into step.

'Rosie Middleton.'

'Rosie . . .' He rolled the 'R'. 'In Spain the diminutive of Rosa is Rosita. My name is José Maria. Is this your first visit to Spain?'

Towards the top of the hill they had to step into a side street to let two cars come past. They were followed by a third vehicle, a Land Rover driven by Nick. He did not see them, his attention being on a couple of small children on his nearside.

'I wonder where Nick is off to. He's supposed to be working this morning,' said Rosie, as the Land Rover passed out of sight.

'There was a bunch of carnations on the passenger seat. I expect he is going to see Señora Clermont,' said José. 'There are only two foreigners living here . . . Nick and the French lady. They are very close friends. She does not have much money. He is very

good to her. Every week flowers...chocolates...wine.'
He smiled. 'Encarna is jealous because Señora
Clermont cooks for Nick and Encarna thinks he likes
her dishes better than Encarna's. Perhaps he does.
They say French food is the best in the world. Is that
true, do you think?'

'I don't think it's possible to compare the cuisines
of different countries which, at their best, are all delicious,' she answered diplomatically. 'Nick says the
bar in Font Vella serves a superb leg of lamb. If
Encarna's cooking is as good as her coffee, I should
think Nick enjoys every mouthful of the food she
cooks for him.'

'She is a very good cook, but he cannot converse
with her as he does with Señora Clermont. She is a
woman of the world who speaks several languages and
can discuss many subjects. They are of equal high in-
tellect . . . is that how you would say it?'

'It would be more idiomatic to say "They are in-
tellectual equals",' she told him.

And what else are they? she wondered. Lovers,
perhaps?

CHAPTER FOUR

WHEN Rosie returned to the monastery she found Carolyn and Anna having a late breakfast at the table on the terrace.

Although the stall-holders and shoppers in the *plaza* were wearing sweaters and cardigans, Rosie had taken hers off and the others were breakfasting in bathing suits. To anyone from northern Europe, the sun was now summer-hot although there was a noticeable drop in temperature in the shade.

'Morning, Rosie. Encarna told us you'd had breakfast with Nick and then gone exploring. Like some more coffee? This is our second pot. I'll go and ask for another cup.' Slipping her arms into a beach wrap, Anna went to the kitchen.

'I hope you didn't keep Nick chatting when he should have been back at his desk,' said Carolyn. 'I don't want our visit to interfere with his routine.'

'It wasn't my idea to have breakfast with him,' said Rosie. 'Afterwards he was going to have a swim and suggested I join him, but I said I'd rather go for a walk round the village.'

'That was sensible of you. It could be all too easy in surroundings like these——' Carolyn indicated the swimming pool which now had its cover removed and four sunbeds and two 'sunbrellas' arranged alongside it '—for him to get out the way of writing at fixed times. You wouldn't believe the trouble I have getting some of my authors to work regular hours and finish their books on schedule.'

Rosie wondered what Carolyn would say if she knew Nick was not in his workroom but taking flowers to a Frenchwoman. But if he had slipped out to a rendezvous when he should have his nose to the grindstone that was his affair—in every sense of the word.

'Yes, writers can be a pain in the neck at times,' Carolyn continued. 'A lot of them treat an editor as a cross between a confessor and a psychiatrist. I've had all kinds of troubles dumped on me . . . not only writer's block but financial and marital difficulties . . . which I've had enough of in my own life,' she added, with a grimace.

Rosie felt this was a cue for her to ask what had gone wrong with Carolyn's marriage. In her experience, people did not refer to aspects of their lives they preferred to forget. But she was not in the mood to give a sympathetic hearing to the other woman's past problems so she said, 'At least you won't get the "My wife doesn't understand me" spiel from Nick.'

'No, thank God. That's a line we've all heard *ad nauseam*,' said Carolyn. 'But I'm sure there've been plenty of women who would have liked to marry him regardless of his being away a lot of the time. When you knew him before, did he have a regular girlfriend?'

'He left the *News* soon after they took me on. He was senior staff, I was a raw recruit. As you can imagine, we didn't have a lot of contact.'

'I suppose not.'

Anna returned with a cup and saucer. As she poured coffee for Rosie, she said, 'I might have still been asleep but the noise of the market below my window woke me up. I'm glad it did. It would have been a pity to waste any of this glorious day. What's the market like, Rosie? Anything worth buying?'

'Not really. I met José Maria and he says the best Spanish pottery comes from Talavera de la Reina but that's a long way from here and most of the stuff they send to the *costas* is tawdry, made for the tourist market. When his mother was young a lot of the women in this village did beautiful needlework but now they watch television. Some women have knitting machines but the days of fine handiwork are gone.'

'Yes, Encarna told me the same thing,' said Anna. 'I asked her about the smocked dresses all the little girls wore on Sundays when John and I honeymooned here. They are still being made but, as the number of needlewomen diminishes, the prices rise. Only rich people can afford them now, she says.'

Presently Rosie went upstairs to put on a black and white two-piece she had bought on a holiday in the Seychelles with Sasha the previous winter. The intervening summer had been wet, with few opportunities to top up the golden tans they had both acquired on that trip. Her body was now back to its natural creamy colour.

After tying a scarf over her hair, she applied a total sun-block to her face. With her colouring she felt it was better to forgo a facial tan in order to conserve what Nick had called her 'lovely skin'.

It was true that she had never suffered from the common adolescent blemishes and even in her teens had been complimented on her complexion. But she was surprised that Nick had noticed her skin and remembered her 'beautiful eyes'. Had he really been struck by them? Or had both remarks been merely what her down-to-earth brothers would call 'a load of flannel'?

'Roly-poly Rosie'. Had that been what they had called her when she was not within hearing? At least, as nicknames went, it had an affectionate ring. And there was nothing roly-poly about her now.

A few minutes ago Anna had been bemoaning her spare tyre and, although she hadn't drawn attention to them, Carolyn had what beauticians called cellulite on her thighs. But, although Rosie would have liked to be a couple of inches taller than her actual height of five feet five, at the moment she had no more problems with her figure.

In fact no problems at all, and that was the way she wanted to keep it.

They were stretched out on the loungers, half asleep in the sun, when Nick's voice said, 'Time for *aperitivos*, girls.'

Shading her eyes with her hand, Rosie saw that he was carrying a tray bearing four tall glasses, a jug of orange juice and a bottle of champagne on ice.

'Have you finished your stint for the day?' Carolyn asked, sitting up and giving a hitch to the top of her emerald strapless one-piece.

'Yes, ma'am. For the rest of the day I'm at your disposal,' he said, with a bow and a smile.

He looked pleased with himself, Rosie thought. Was it because he had spent the morning in the arms of his mistress?

'You said you would make a copy of your CV for me,' she reminded him.

'Here it is.' He put down the tray and handed her some pages of typescript inside a transparent plastic pocket.

'Thank you.' She was surprised he had remembered.

Nick filled the glasses with Buck's Fizz and handed them round. His long legs were already exposed by his khaki shorts. Now he took off his T-shirt.

The play of muscle under his deeply tanned skin as he tugged it over his head and tossed it over the back of the fourth sunbed stirred an involuntary flutter in the pit of her stomach. She looked away, knowing what she felt was not just an aesthetic response to the beauty of the human body in splendid condition.

Anna, whose lounger was next to his, reached out an arm for the T-shirt. He had already turned it the right way out and her eye had been caught by a logo on the front.

'"Costa Blanca Mountain Walkers' Club",' she read out. '"*Hacia arriba*" . . . which means "To the top"—yes?'

He nodded. 'There are some fine walks in the mountains along this coast but it isn't a good idea to go off alone. Accidents can happen and on the more remote tracks that could be serious. When I first came to Spain there were old men and mules using a lot of the tracks, and many of the isolated *casitas* were still in use if not actually inhabited. Since then the drift from the land has made it advisable to walk the mountains with a companion or in a group. Have you tried the pool? Is the temperature warm enough for you?'

'Carolyn and I have wallowed a couple of times. Rosie's the only good swimmer. She's like a dolphin in the water.'

'That remark is a typical bit of publicity director's hype,' said Rosie, smiling at Anna. 'I'm an average swimmer, but I do enjoy it.' She tucked a strand of still-wet hair behind her ear and hoped she was not going to blush because Nick's blue eyes were scanning her body.

Her two-piece had been chosen for active swimming, not to show off her figure, but under his slow appraisal it suddenly felt much more scanty than it had before he joined them.

Referring to their earlier conversation, he said, 'Buxom is definitely not applicable any more. Svelte is the word I'd choose now if I were composing a handout about you.'

'Rosie writes a very good press release,' said Anna. 'It's not easy to avoid the clichés of our trade, but she always manages to come up with something fresh.'

Carolyn said, 'Are your characters based on real people, Nick, or are they pure invention?'

'Surely the imagination is like a computer? Nothing can come out which hasn't been fed in,' he answered. 'But the mind is so extremely complex that it's impossible to trace the source of every idea or image it produces. I believe everything in fiction must have its origin in fact, but the facts may have been stored and forgotten for years and so muddled up with other facts that what emerges is quite different from what went in.'

A little later, when he had dived into the pool and was having a vigorous swim before lunch, Anna said, 'I think the women in *Crusade* must be based on people he's known. They were too true to life not to be ... especially the French girl.'

Until that moment Rosie had not connected the French girl called Laure in the book with Nick's close friend Madame Clermont here at Font Vella. But now, all at once, she felt certain that Anna was right.

The girl in the book was too original, too inherently feminine not to have been drawn from life. Nick could never have invented her. Laure had to be a thinly disguised portrait of someone he knew, someone with whom he had been—was still, it appeared—on the most intimate terms.

The realisation was so unpleasant, so much like having the contents of the ice bucket chucked over her, that in a flash of enlightenment she knew she had never really got over her youthful infatuation.

All these years, deep in her heart, she had remained in love with him, or rather with the way she had wanted him to be. No real man had ever matched up to that idealised version of Nick. No man ever could, unless she could find a way to get Nick out of her system.

She watched him reach the far end of the pool, put his hands flat on the sun-baked tiles round the edge and, with an easy movement which flexed every sinew of his broad, powerful back, swing himself out of the water.

As he strolled back to where they were sitting, his wet hair looking as black as José's as he raked it back from his forehead, rivulets of water coursing down the smoothly sculpted planes of his body, she wondered if the only way to destroy, finally and completely, her long-dormant feelings for him was to have an affair with him.

If she threw herself at him, would he take her?

* * *

At one o'clock Encarna appeared with a tray of *tapas*.
Lunch would not be served until three.

By now the sun was so hot it was impossible to
believe that, only a short flight away from where they
were basking, people were wearing overcoats and
probably using umbrellas.

'But it can be cold and wet here at times in the
winter,' said Nick, when Carolyn remarked that it was
a wonder anyone lived in northern Europe when they
could be enjoying this climate.

The *tapas* included three different kinds of olives,
pickled anchovies, thin slices of a sausage called
chorizo, snippets of mountain-cured ham and a dip
served in spoonfuls on the heart leaves from an endive.

'But this isn't Spanish,' said Nick, urging them to
try it. 'Encarna makes this under duress because it's
a French idea and she's not keen on the French.'

'Why not?' asked Carolyn.

He shrugged. 'Irrational prejudice.'

'Does she know any French people?' Rosie asked,
curious to see what he would say.

'Only one...the Frenchwoman who showed her how
to make these *bouchées* which, being very touchy in
some ways, Encarna took as an implied criticism of
the nibbles she provides. In fact Marie-Laure is a
charming woman. She would have enjoyed meeting
you but unfortunately she's in the Benidorm Clinic
for a minor op at the moment.'

So her supposition had been right, thought Rosie,
with a pang. He had even used part of his inamorata's
name for the character she had inspired.

'I've never heard the name Encarna before. Is it
common in Spain?' Anna asked.

'Not as common as Maria and Carmen, but not uncommon,' Nick told her. 'A Spanish girl's name I like is Nieves, from the word meaning "snows". I've called the girl in my second book Snow, but I'm not sure that in English it doesn't sound affected. What do you think?'

Rosie wondered if Snow was based on a Spanish girlfriend he had had.

Carolyn said. 'I like it. It's original...at least I don't think it's been used before, apart from Snow-White in the fairy-tale. I think you may have hit on a name as unusual and memorable as Margaret Mitchell's stroke of genius with Scarlett.'

'There might be a shout-line in that,' Anna said thoughtfully.

'What's a shout-line?' he asked.

'A line for the cover of a book or for an advertisement. It might be something straightforward like "best-selling author of *Crusade*" on the jacket of your next book. Or it could be something on the lines of "Snow...the most compelling heroine since Scarlett O'Hara", although that would be more suitable for a novel for women than for your books aimed at men.'

'They may be aimed at men but I think they'll be bought by both sexes. Women may skip some of the technical bits, but they'll lap up the love scenes,' said Carolyn. She looked at Rosie. 'Don't you agree? If you'd dipped into the book and read one of the scenes Laure is in, wouldn't you have bought the book?'

'Probably, but whether I dipped into the book would depend on the jacket. If the jacket says, in effect, this is a man's book—if it has a gun and a hypodermic needle on the cover—a lot of women won't bother even to dip.'

'I hope I can get that across to Colin,' said Carolyn. 'He's our Art Director,' she explained to Nick. 'He deals with the covers of all our mega-lead titles. The also-rans are left to his assistants.'

The discussion continued until lunch, eaten in the garden, at a table under a canopy of thin canes tied to a frame which, in summer, was covered by the leaves of a *parra* which, Nick explained, was a climbing grape vine.

After lunch he went to his workroom to fill in the questionnaire Anna had given him and the women returned to the sunbeds, Anna and Carolyn to have an outdoor siesta and Rosie to study the CV he had given her earlier.

It revealed some things she had not known, such as the fact that he was the son of a diplomat and had been born in Washington DC. It gave details of his education and the names of the four newspapers he had worked on before turning to television. It said that his leisure interests included reading, rock climbing, sailing, snorkelling and music. It listed the countries to which he had travelled for work and pleasure.

But although it made him sound an interesting man, it did not convey his magnetism. Only a photograph could do that. It wasn't that he was handsome in the strict sense of the word. No man who had had the cartilage below the high bridge of his nose punched slightly out of shape in a schoolboys' fight, and whose forehead still bore the scar of a glancing blow from a stone hurled in a Middle East fracas, could be described as handsome. His were the rugged looks of an outdoors man, a born adventurer and risk-taker, not the somewhat effeminate face of a male model or a popular heart-throb.

Suddenly restless, Rosie put the CV aside and, moving softly so as not to disturb the two who were dozing, she tied the large square of Indian Paisley-printed cotton she used as a beach wrap over her swimsuit. Then, barefoot, she left the pool area and wandered around the large garden, an idea for a press release beginning to form in her mind.

The garden's paths were laid with old clay tiles which were pleasant to walk on. Here and there among the fruit trees and ornamental shrubs, an enormous earthenware jar, which had once contained olive oil and was large enough to hide a man of Nick's size, lay on its side. At various vantage points there were seats of weathered cedar or stone to sit on while enjoying the view.

Under the drooping lace-like branches of what she knew was a false pepper tree because there was another near the pool and Anna had asked him the name of it during lunch, Rosie sat sideways on a bench with her feet on it and her arms clasped round her knees, a favourite position for sessions of creative thought.

She wished she had her files with her. Because there was a part of her which would always be a journalist, and occasionally there were moments when she regretted deserting her first career for PR, she often filed and re-read articles by journalists she admired.

Thinking about arresting ways to introduce Nick to the Press, the book trade and the public, had reminded her of a guess-who game which gave unusual insights into a person's character. One game-player would think of a famous person, and then everyone else would ask: if this person were an item of furniture, what would he or she be? If this person were a drink, what would she or he be? And so on until somebody guessed the person's identity.

Might it not be an intriguing way to present Nick?

If this man were a sweet he would be plain dark chocolate. If he were a drink he would be extra dry *cava*. If he were——

'Rosie?'

This time Nick did not catch her off guard. She heard him calling her name, but not loudly, before he came into view round the edge of the crescent-shaped cypress hedge which screened her seat.

'Ah, there you are! I've just had a message from London for some people who live in the *campo* and don't have a telephone. It's not far...half an hour there and back. Would you like to come and see a bit of the countryside?'

As she could see many miles of countryside from where she was sitting and would not have as good a view from inside the Land Rover, she thought he must have another reason for inviting her to go with him.

Still torn between sticking to her original intention to spend as little time *à deux* with him as possible, and her more recent thought that perhaps the only way to exorcise him from her heart was to offer herself to him on a plate, she hesitated.

'If you'd rather stay here, don't agree to come out of politeness. I've already got the message that our reunion doesn't please you as much as it does me,' he said drily.

'That's rather a curious statement. You had forgotten my existence.'

'No, I hadn't. As a matter of fact you have quite often been in my mind during the years since I left the *News*.'

'That I do *not* believe!' she said flatly. 'Why on earth should you remember a teenage junior reporter who was only there for a short time before you left? I shouldn't put it past you to have forgotten Di Preston.'

For some seconds he looked at her blankly, not troubling to hide that at first all memory of the sub-editor's wife with whom he had had an affair eluded him.

'You see? If you can't remember a woman you went to bed with, you can't convince me that you remembered me.'

Irritated by his attempt to soft-soap her, but much more deeply vexed by her own folly in wanting him, she swung her feet to the ground and stood up, intending to walk away.

Nick prevented her departure with a hand on her shoulder. The unexpected physical contact of his palm on her bare shoulder made her draw in her breath.

'You shouldn't be walking about with bare feet. There may be thorns and sharp bits of grit on the path and you have soft soles,' he said.

Before she could say that the paths looked well-swept to her, he astounded her by dropping his hand from her shoulder and picking her up.

'What the hell...?' Rosie protested.

'You're a featherweight now. I shouldn't have wanted to carry you far ten years ago,' he said, smiling.

'Put me down, Nick,' she said crossly, her heart beating wildly at being held in his arms.

'I don't want those pretty feet hurt.' He was openly teasing her, amused by her discomfiture.

'If you don't put me down, one of your pretty blue eyes will get blacked,' she said furiously, horrified at the strength of her reaction to being cradled against his chest.

'Try it and see what happens to you,' was Nick's mocking reply. 'I think I have more experience in the art of unarmed combat than you have, Rosie. Not that I would dream of hurting you. There are other ways of subduing an aggressive woman . . . if she's as attractive as you are.' His gaze shifted to her mouth. 'The last time you were in my arms, you seemed to like it.'

CHAPTER FIVE

FOR THE first time in her life Rosie experienced an extraordinary split between her mind and her body: her mind raging that he should twit her about the time he had kissed her—the first male ever to kiss her on the lips; her body melting and quivering with longing for him to do it again.

And he would have kissed her, of that she was certain. Except that just as the glint of mockery in his eyes changed to a different kind of gleam, Anna came round the hedge from the other side.

'Oops... sorry. I should have knocked,' she said, disappearing.

'It's all right, Anna. No need for a discreet exit,' said Nick, following her. 'I'm holding Rosie because she walked here without shoes and I think it's unwise to patter around barefoot.'

'Oh... I see,' said Anna.

She did not look as if she believed him. Rosie wondered if she had heard the tail-end of what they had been saying and might even have butted in deliberately, disapproving of someone engaged to provide his PR getting sexually involved with a B & P author.

She could change her mind and drop me from this assignment, thought Rosie, in sudden panic.

'Nick, stop fooling... put me down,' she said in a low urgent tone, as Anna walked on ahead of them.

'Stop fussing,' he answered firmly. 'If you walk around barefoot overseas you could get a nasty infection from a parasite which burrows into feet. I always wear flip-flops except on clean beaches, and so should you.'

From then until they were back in the pool area she maintained a mutinous silence, furious with him, furious with Anna for intruding on them, whether by accident or intention, furious with herself.

Fortunately Carolyn had gone indoors and did not see them return, although Anna might tell her what had happened.

'Thank you,' Rosie said frigidly, when Nick set her on her feet. 'Your concern was quite unnecessary but no doubt you meant well.' As Anna wasn't watching, she flashed him an arctic look which she hoped masked the fact that her heart was still pumping at twice its normal rate.

Without further reference to his invitation of a few minutes earlier, Nick said, 'I have to go out for a short time. When I get back, if you like I'll take you all on a tour of the village. It has one or two interesting features, particularly the ceramic pictures on the Stations of the Cross leading up to the Calvary.'

'Thank you, Nick. We'd like that.' When he had gone, Anna said, 'Do I gather that you and Nick had something going way back when you worked on the same paper? He'd like to rake up the ashes, but you wouldn't: have I got it right?'

'No, you're miles off,' said Rosie. 'There was nothing between us, unless you count a peck under the mistletoe at an editorial staff Christmas party. Nick was the office heart-throb. You heard him call me Roly-Poly Rosie at dinner last night. You might not think it now, but thanks to Mum's cooking I was a walking, talking tub of farm butter.'

'Some men like plenty to cuddle. He remembered your beautiful eyes. It makes no odds to me if you two want to tango,' said Anna. 'I don't think Carolyn will like it. She fancies him herself.'

'And is welcome to him,' said Rosie. 'You've known me some time, Anna. You know my work comes first with me.'

'It has up to now. I don't suppose it will forever. Sooner or later we all come to the point when the most important thing in the world is a man. It may not last long but it happens, even to women who don't need the opposite sex for any reason but the biological one. I doubt if you're immune. I thought I was, but I wasn't once John came on the scene.'

'John works in London. You might not have succumbed to him if it had meant resigning your job and going off to live in some remote spot like this,' said Rosie. 'I wonder if Carolyn has considered that.'

'That wouldn't put her off. Don't be misled by the fact that she's a first-rate editor. She's only dedicated to her career as long as she needs it to pay the rent and the grocery bill. She would pack it in tomorrow if a rich author asked her to confine her skills to his books. Nick is tailor-made for her.'

It was on the tip of Rosie's tongue to tell Anna she had reason to believe that everything Nick needed from the opposite sex was provided by the Frenchwoman who had inspired the sexy, witty character called Laure in his book.

He might not consider himself bound to her. He might have a fling with someone else if he felt like it. But Rosie could not see him starting a long-term relationship with Carolyn or anyone else while the model for Laure was conveniently close at hand.

Later when they were setting out to tour the village, she said, 'Where does Font Vella's other foreigner live—the Frenchwoman you mentioned this morning? Shall we be passing her house?'

'Yes, it has a particularly attractive shrine to the Virgin in an alcove in the façade.'

Half an hour later, when they came to Madame Clermont's house with its blue-robed, gold-crowned statuette set in a niche with a glass door, he said, 'It's a pity I can't show you the interior of the house. Marie-Laure has left me her key but I can't take you inside without her permission. She has impeccable taste and gave me a lot of advice about furnishing the monastery on a shoestring before I had enough money to give Parladé a free hand.'

'How long has she lived here?' Rosie asked.

'Ten years. Font Vella has never had as many houses for sale as some villages. There are places with as many as twenty foreigners—possibly more—living in them. But this village looks like remaining predominantly Spanish for some time to come. Which is how both she and I like it.'

So their relationship must have lasted for several years, Rosie thought, as they moved on towards the bar where Nick ordered one of the renowned roasts to be prepared for their lunch the following day.

When they returned to the monastery, Carolyn said, 'May we see your study or is it strictly private?'

'Certainly you may see it.' He led the way to a room with a large map of the world on one wall and on another a chart showing what he called the bones of his current book.

'I'd rather you didn't look at that, if you don't mind,' he said pleasantly. 'It may be eccentric of me, but I like to keep my plots and characters under hatches until the book is finished.'

Carolyn looked faintly disapproving, Rosie thought. No doubt she would have liked to be consulted at every stage, although Rosie remembered a woman writer whom she had taken on tour telling her that she never discussed her novels with anyone because, if she did, the compulsion to put it on paper was lost.

'You had this custom-made, I imagine?' said Anna, looking at the desk bearing his computer and printer, a facsimile machine, an answering machine and various other gadgets.

'The village *carpintero* made it up to my design.'

Remembering what she had been thinking about when he joined her behind the cypress hedge, and, seeing that his computer was the same as her own, Rosie said, 'You haven't got a spare disk you would let me use to knock some ideas into shape, have you? Like most computer addicts I find it quite hard to work with any more primitive system now.'

'I know what you mean,' he said. 'I find the words never flow as well if for some reason I'm forced to use a typewriter. As for writing with pencil and paper...perish the thought! By all means use the machine. I'll program it for you. I take it you know this system?'

When the others had disappeared through the jib-door to the library, Rosie settled herself in his comfortable working chair and tapped out the thoughts she had had in the garden earlier.

Then she typed, 'If this person were a tree he would be...? Leaving the end of the line blank, she sat back to ponder how to complete the clue.

She had just typed in 'umbrella pine' when Nick came back with a mug in his hand.

'I can't remember if you take sugar.'

'I used to. I don't any more. Thank you.'

Expecting him to rejoin the others, she was disconcerted when he slung a long thigh over the end of the desk which had no equipment on it and stretched out his other leg.

'By the way, in the interests of accuracy, I never went to bed with Di Preston.'

At the end of a long pause, she said, 'You may not have done so, literally. Are you trying to make me believe you never made love to her anywhere?'

'You can only change people's minds if their minds are open. I'm not sure that yours is . . . as far as I'm concerned, Rosie.'

'That's dodging the question.'

'Then I'll be unchivalrous and tell you that, in spite of being given a great deal of encouragement, I did not respond to Mrs Preston's advances, which were largely motivated by a desire to serve her gander the same sauce he had served her. She convinced him and you and no doubt a lot of other people that she and I were what is crudely called "having it off". We were not.'

He rose. 'Believe it or not, as you please. It's the truth.' He began to walk towards the door.

He had almost reached it when she said, 'Wait a minute, Nick.'

He paused, turning his head and raising an enquiring eyebrow.

Rosie said, 'I believe it. Why should you bother to lie to me? It's not my business anyway. I'm sorry I misjudged you.'

'I'm sorry someone was sufficiently mean-minded to plant that unpleasant disillusionment in your idealistic head. I may be wrong, but I think you probably had a bit of a schoolgirl crush on me.'

Not for the first time on this trip, Rosie found herself torn by conflicting impulses. She was tempted to deny it and equally tempted to admit, with a nonchalance appropriate to a sophisticated woman of twenty-seven admitting to something which had happened too long ago to be anything but a joke now, that in those far off days she had been crazy about him.

Instead she said, 'I think I was exceptionally naïve for my age. At the time it was rather upsetting to be told that the first man to kiss me was anything but a *parfit gentil knight*. My parents married quite young and I'm sure my father has never wanted anyone but Mum or she anyone but him. When you grow up as part of a large self-sufficient country family, you form ideas about love and marriage which are different from most people's. I've changed a lot of my ideas since then, but I'm still not impressed by womanisers.'

'And do you see me in that light?'

'You're thirty-five, heterosexual but not married. You may live in a monastery but I doubt if you live the celibate life of your predecessors here. I should think chastity has as little place in your life as poverty.'

'I haven't lived like a monk,' he agreed. 'Have you lived like a nun? If so, you must have extraordinary will-power to resist all the approaches which must have been made to you.'

'I didn't resist love when it was offered to me...and I thought I could return it.'

'But it didn't last, hm?'

'No, unfortunately not.'

'How long ago did it break up?'

She tapped a light tattoo on the edge of the keyboard. 'I'm here on business, Nick, not to discuss my private life.'

'Hint taken. I'll leave you in peace.' He rose and went out of the room.

Not in peace, thought Rosie, as she sipped the tea. Her peace of mind had evaporated the night Anna had rung up about him.

What ought she to do? Keep him firmly at arm's length? Or be friendly, warm, responsive and see what, if anything, developed?

It wasn't like her to vacillate. Up to now, with all the major decisions in her life, she had seen clearly what she should do and done it. The decision to drop her plan to try magazine work and take the PR opportunity had not kept her awake at night. Nor had the beginning and ending of her last long relationship caused her days of uncertainty.

But now, thrown together with her first love, her normal clarity of mind was clouded by emotion and indecision.

Before, 'not knowing which way to turn' had been merely an expression, not a situation she had experienced. Now the phrase described exactly how she felt, and to someone of her even, orderly temperament it was as alien as living in an untidy muddle or having a dusty, cluttered desk.

Nick's desk was as workmanlike as her own desks at the office and in her bedroom in Fulham. But although he was using all the latest forms of technology and, she noticed, had even invested in a large commercial-size photocopier, there were some personal touches among all the up-to-date gadgetry.

The mug in which he kept his pens, pencils and highlighters looked as if it might be an example of the Talavera pottery José had told her about. His letter opener combined a stiletto-sharp blade with the ornate silver handle seen on antique button-hooks. Perhaps it had been a present from Marie-Laure Clermont. It looked like the kind of practical yet decorative gift a woman of taste might devise for her lover.

The baskets of finely woven grass and cane which were evidently IN and OUT trays had probably been picked up by Nick on his travels in the East, as no doubt had the lapiz shell box in which he kept his stamps. She could see the head of King Juan Carlos through the semi-transparent shell.

She worked on her ideas until Anna put her head round the door. 'Take a break to look at a gorgeous sunset over the mountains. We're watching it from the *mirador* opposite our bedrooms. Better hurry if you want to see it. It won't last long.'

Rosie closed the document she was working on and removed from the machine the small floppy disk Nick had given her. Replacing its plastic cover, she put it in her pocket. At this stage she did not want Nick to see her incomplete ideas.

Perhaps, as he had sufficient faith in her integrity to leave her with access to all his private files, she should trust him not to sneak a look at her notes. He was going to see what she had written about him sooner or later.

Passing the complicated chart with its jigsaw of coloured labels with notes written on them, she wondered if Carolyn, left alone in his study, would be able to resist looking at it.

She found the others sitting on canvas directors' chairs set out in the upper cloister where Nick had found her that morning. Now, the sun having already sunk behind the half-circle of mountains, their rugged crests were in dark silhouette against a sky blazing with every shade of red from crimson to pale pink with, here and there, streaks of apricot and mother-of-pearl.

'This doesn't happen every night,' said Nick. 'We're drinking vodka and tonic. Is that all right for you, Rosie?'

'I'll have tonic by itself, if I may, please?'

'Of course.' When he brought it to where she was sitting, as he put it into her hand, he bent to say quietly, 'You haven't got a headache, have you?'

'No, I'm fine. I'm just giving my liver a short rest,' she said, with a smile.

He nodded. 'I asked because sometimes people get headaches, even migraines, when they come here and relax from their usual rat-race.'

He returned to his chair on the far side of the two in which the others were sitting.

Anna, who had heard what he said, leaned forward slightly to speak to him across Carolyn.

'I should have thought you might have had a problem getting your house guests to go back to the rat-race after a taste of this idyllic life.'

'It's not always as good as today,' he said drily. 'Today has been Spain at its best. The mountains can look pretty bleak with rain-clouds hanging over them, and eight power-cuts in a day are exasperating to anyone using a computer. But I guess a sunset like this is worth a fair bit of aggro.'

'I think it's sheer heaven here,' said Carolyn. 'To be honest, I'd thought of Spain as completely ruined by hordes of the worst type of tourists ... except in the really remote parts, and I'm not keen on camping and hiking. *This* to me is perfection. I should adore to have a place here—not on the grand scale you have, Nick, but a cottage to come to for long weekends when I really needed to unwind. Is there any chance of finding one?'

Anna flicked a swift glance at Rosie, who interpreted it to mean, What did I tell you?

Nick said, 'Not in Font Vella. You might find something in one of the other *pueblos*. You'd have to go to an estate agent to find out what is available.'

'But your French friend has a house here. Surely, sooner or later, others must come on the market? Not all old people have children to leave their houses to. Young couples move away to get better jobs. If anything did come up, you'd be among the first to hear of it, wouldn't you?'

'Probably. Encarna knows everyone's business and usually relays it to me. But if any houses are going to be sold, I am now—thanks to Bury & Poole's substantial advance—in a position to buy them.'

'You already have this great place. Why do you want more houses?'

'To save them from being badly done up. Also, I don't want to live in a village where some of the houses stand empty most of the time.'

He rose to hand round a dish of olives.

'A few years ago,' he went on, 'when the English began buying property in northern France, the French saw a danger of certain picturesque towns being virtually taken over by foreigners, most of them not full-time residents. The danger exists here. There are places where it has happened. I would sell a house to you, Carolyn, only if you wanted to live in the village and speak Spanish to your neighbours. Not if you came here occasionally, bought all your supplies at one of the big supermarkets on the coast, and mixed exclusively with other foreigners.'

Carolyn's full lips formed a reproachful mock pout. 'I should have thought you might make an exception in my case,' she said archly. 'You wouldn't have got such a large advance if I hadn't said I'd resign if I couldn't have *carte blanche* to outbid everyone else who wanted *Crusade.*'

'I'm delighted you have such confidence in the book, but I'm afraid it's not possible to return the compliment by promising you the chance to buy the first house which comes up. You were backing your judgement with company money. I have a more personal stake in the future of this village.'

Rosie, in Carolyn's place, would have smiled, agreed, left it at that. The fiction director had a stronger strain of persistence in her make-up.

She said, 'I'm beginning to think you're as implacable as Jake in *Crusade*. Not many editors would have laid their jobs on the line for you.'

Nick looked amused. 'I'm sure there was never much risk that your resignation would be accepted. When I began asking around among the people I knew who knew about publishing, your name was always high on the list of the best people in it, Carolyn.' He looked at the sky. 'The show's over. Shall we go down?'

That night they had bowls of vegetable broth followed by cold cuts for supper. After serving the soup, Encarna went home to watch television. When the meal was over they all helped to clear the table and load the dishwasher.

Then, for the second time, they sat round a fire of logs cut from old olive trees. Nick had a television which he said had been useful when he was perfecting his Spanish but which now he rarely watched.

'Some of the foreigners here—Americans as well as Brits—have satellite dishes installed so that they can see US and UK programmes,' he said, handing round cups of coffee. 'But there's nowhere I could put a dish without spoiling the look of the building or the garden.'

He was pouring out liqueurs for everyone but Rosie, who didn't want to get back to London and find that her weight was up several pounds, when Anna said suddenly, 'I've had a brainwave.'

They all looked expectantly at her.

'Do you remember, Rosie, how before *Mistral's Daughter* was published a planeload of people was flown to Provence to have lunch with Judith Krantz? Another time a bunch of sales reps flew to Jersey for a champagne party at Jack Higgins' place. I think we should go one better... well, actually *two* better.'

She paused and Rosie, with a premonitory inkling of what was in Anna's mind, felt her spirits sink.

'If we can find a hotel with suitable facilities, we should start by holding the sales conference here on the Costa Blanca,' Anna announced. 'Then we should bring the wholesalers down and have a party for them at El Monasterio. You wouldn't mind that, would you, Nick?'

Taking his assent for granted, she went on, 'Later, before publication, we'll charter a third plane to bring down a load of literary editors. With an author who lives in surroundings like these, it would be crazy not to cash in on them.'

'You're right: it's a marvellous idea,' Carolyn agreed.

Nick said, 'There are several suitable hotels. That's no problem. But I don't think Rosie shares your enthusiasm.'

From the opposite side of the hearth his blue eyes met her troubled grey ones. 'Why not, Rosie?'

She had a disturbing conviction that he already knew why not.

CHAPTER SIX

'ON THE contrary, I can't think of a better way to get the people who matter interested in and behind the book,' she replied.

Which was true. In her professional capacity, she gave Anna's plan full marks. It was only the inner self, the once bruised and still vulnerable heart at the core of Rosalind Middleton, PR consultant, who had reservations and misgivings in so far as the proposal affected her.

'Good. Then I think tomorrow morning, while you're working, Nick, Rosie and I should check out some possible venues for the conference,' said Anna. 'The conference for the spring list is held in November which, being out of season, means that it should be possible to get very favourable rates for a block booking. Would it be wise to order a taxi tonight? Would you like to come with us, Carolyn?'

'You're the experts in that sphere. I'd sooner stay here and go through my notes on *Crusade* ready to start work with Nick when you two go back on Monday,' said his editor.

Rosie's sense of humour, normally more in evidence than it had been so far this weekend, suddenly prompted her to make a suggestion which might jolt Nick a bit.

'Why not go the whole hog and run a competition open to all female bookshop staff, the major prize being a weekend with Nick at El Monasterio,' she suggested. 'There've often been competitions for the best window display of a specific title. Don't you think a contest for saleswomen, the first prize going to the one who sells the highest number of copies of *Crusade* in the first two weeks after publication, would be more effective?'

It was Carolyn who objected. 'It's a bit much to expect Nick to play host to some unknown female who may be a crashing bore,' she said.

'Journalists never find anyone a bore,' Rosie told her. 'Everyone has something interesting about them. It's a matter of asking the right questions. Isn't it, Nick?' She gave him a bland smile.

He smiled back at her. 'It's a good idea, but why confine it to saleswomen? Why not any bookshop staff, with the winner entitled to bring their partner or a friend? That way, if they find me a bore, they've got each other to talk to.'

It was terribly hard not to like him, she thought, with unwilling admiration for his quick and good-humoured riposte. How many people of his standing would suggest, even in fun, that they might be boring to some? Not many. Very few of the VIPs with whom she had had dealings.

She wondered if Nick's present attitude would survive being number one in the bestseller charts for months on end, for there was no doubt in her mind that that was where *Crusade* would be soon after its publication.

Perhaps success wouldn't change him; he had, after all, been successful in two fields already. But bestseller-dom was different. Some writers began to believe their own publicity and become insufferably big-headed and arrogant.

But maybe Marie-Laure Clermont would keep his feet on the ground in the way that Laure in the book kept the hero, Jake, from losing his sense of perspective.

The next morning Anna and Rosie went to look over the state-owned *parador* at Jávea and two ordinary hotels on the coast Nick had suggested.

By the time they got back to the monastery he had finished his morning stint and joined Carolyn by the pool.

'How did you get on?' she asked them, looking more than usually pleased with life.

Rosie felt sure Nick must have been flirting with her. How could one like a man who exerted his charm on other women when his mistress wasn't around? she thought, vexed at the memory of warming to him the night before. In her book, a decent man was as faithful to his current *amour* as he should be to a wife. Men who saw the entire female sex as a kind of huge harem were anathema to her.

When they arrived at the bar where they were having lunch it was full of local family groups, all of them including a grandparent or elderly relation as well as small children and babies. Rosie had already noticed that the old people in Spain were much shorter in stature than their descendants, which Nick said was because anyone over sixty had probably not had enough to eat as a child. The horrors and privations of the Civil War were still within living memory and Spain's poverty had been relieved only by the coming of tourism.

A corner table for four was reserved for them and, as Nick led the way to it, he was hailed with unmis-

takable warmth by a number of locals, one old man
in Sunday best actually grasping his arm with stubby
fingers with soil under the nails and making what was
clearly some ribald comment about Nick's having
three women in tow.

Carolyn and Anna, accustomed to eating in the best
restaurants in London, looked rather taken aback by
the simplicity of this establishment where the tables
were covered with white paper, no side plates were
provided and the cutlery was of some cheap dull metal.

Rosie too was accustomed to lunching in plusher
surroundings but, with her back to the wall and a good
view of the crowded room, she found the scene extremely entertaining.

Earthenware jugs of red and white wine were
brought by a teenage boy, the youngest son of the
proprietor, and his sister, also in her teens, brought
a large dish of salad which Nick dressed with oil and
vinegar from glass containers with a wooden stand.

'The form is to leave the salad on the big plate while
everyone digs in,' he said. 'But if you would like me
to ask for salad plates I will.'

'No, no... when in Rome,' said Carolyn brightly,
spreading a small paper napkin over the lap of an
expensive wool dress with a matching shawl thrown
over one shoulder and secured by a dramatic brooch.

Rosie had thought that for lunch in a village bar
jeans and a sweater would be appropriate. But in fact
Carolyn's outfit was more in keeping with the clothes
worn by the local women, who were all got up to the
nines with their hair set and their nails varnished.

After the salad came the large leg of lamb brought
to the table by the proprietor himself—his wife could
be glimpsed through a hatch between the dining area

and the white-tiled kitchen—in a pan full of sizzling juices.

He carved the leg for them, expertly slicing the succulent meat of an animal which had spent its short life grazing on mountain vegetation, including many herbs.

Only that morning, on their way to the coast, Anna and Rosie had seen a herd of sheep and some goats being led across a main road cutting through olive groves by a *pastor* who, although not old, had the deeply weathered face of a man who spent all his life in the open minding his flock.

Having grown up in a farming community, at one time Rosie hadn't questioned the morality of animals being reared for human consumption. But Sasha had always had scruples and Clare too was repelled by modern farming methods. Now they had an agreement not to buy for their own consumption any meat or poultry which had been factory-farmed.

But Rosie could see no harm in eating a sheep which would not have existed at all if it had not been bred for the table and which, from what she had seen of the herd browsing contentedly on the weeds among the olives, led a natural life if a short one.

The lamb was accompanied by a dish of mashed potatoes encrusted with roasted almonds, and the wine in the jugs—she chose the red—was a robust local plonk dry enough to complement the richness of the meat.

'My God! The noise level in here! It must be well over a hundred decibels,' Anna exclaimed, raising her own voice to be heard above the babel of animated Valenciano being spoken at the surrounding tables.

'Yes, Sunday is not the best day to eat out,' said Nick, his own deep, resonant timbre being one of the assets he had brought to the job of TV reporting. 'But if I had brought you here yesterday, when it would have been quieter, Encarna would have been offended. I could have asked her to change her day off, but I knew her family were coming to see her today.'

That was considerate of him, thought Rosie. Some affluent bachelors of her acquaintance didn't give a thought to the convenience of the people who attended to their comfort.

The bar did not offer a large selection of puddings. There was ice-cream and crème caramel or fresh fruit. They chose to finish the meal with oranges and coffee.

'That was delicious but I must say it's rather a relief to get out of that hubbub,' said Anna to Rosie, as they walked back to the monastery, a short distance behind the other two.

Having unlocked his front door, Nick said, 'If you wouldn't mind amusing yourself for a couple of hours, I have an errand to run. I'll be back by sundown. I've asked a few friends in for drinks. It's not often people around here get the chance to talk to three dashing career girls. It would be selfish to keep you to myself.'

He didn't say where he was going but Rosie had little doubt that it was to visit Madame Clermont in the clinic at Benidorm.

Nick's drinks guests were three couples: American, Swedish and a Canadian man with a Dutch wife.

Although all the men were retired, they had led interesting lives and now had sufficient means to travel and enjoy life.

Chatting to the American wife, Rosie couldn't resist asking, 'Do you know Madame Clermont who lives in the village?'

'Marie-Laure? Oh, sure. She's a great gal. Too bad you won't get to meet her. She's in the clinic right now. She's due to come out on Wednesday, but you'll have gone by then. She has the prettiest house you ever saw. Tiny compared with this place, but to tell you the truth I'd rather have her little dolls' house than this great barn of Nick's. It's a showplace, I know, but too big for my taste. I don't know how Encarna keeps it as nice as she does. Most Spanish maids aren't all that efficient. They flick around with those funny little chamois mops, but I don't consider them thorough. My Amparo just hates using the vacuum cleaner. She'd rather sweep with a brush the way her grandmother did.'

Nick came over and said, 'I hope you won't mind if I break up this tête-à-tête. Rosie hasn't met Steve and Joke yet.' He took her lightly by the elbow to lead her away.

'Next time you're here you must come and see our place. It's been nice talking to you,' said the American woman, smiling and turning to join in her husband's conversation with Anna.

Taking Rosie to another part of the room, Nick said, 'I hope I was right to break that up. She's a nice woman but inclined to dwell on matters domestic. She would rather live in the States but Chuck tells me it would cost twice as much to keep his boat there as it does here. He's mad about sailing.'

The visitors stayed a couple of hours. Then, insisting that they relax by the fire, Nick went to organise what he called a scratch supper.

'I'm going to give him a hand,' said Carolyn, a few minutes later.

'I'm going to stay here and enjoy being waited on,' said Anna. 'John is a lot more capable than some men but even so I expect I'll find quite a bit of cleaning up to do when I get back tomorrow.'

'I shan't find that, but I'm quite happy to be lazy and let them do the work,' said Rosie.

They discussed the people they had just met.

'I can't understand Americans wanting to live here when the United States offers such marvellous places to retire to,' said Anna.

'You've worked there, haven't you?'

'Yes…had a fabulous time. I'd be there now except that John's job isn't transferable. If it weren't for the American influence, English publishing would be the cottage industry it still was when I got my first job sixteen years ago.'

Shop talk kept them chatting in comfortable idleness until the others returned with trays of rather more substantial *tapas* than they had before dinner on the night of their arrival.

Carolyn had changed again for the drinks party and was looking very nice in silk jersey trousers and a knitted silk sweater with beads applied to the cable pattern down the front.

Would she meet Nick's Marie-Laure? Rosie wondered. Or would he make a point of keeping it from the 'great gal' that his English editor was a young and attractive divorcée?

The shop talk continued while they ate. Both Anna and Carolyn had a fund of amusing anecdotes about their experiences in the world of publishing with all its in-house rivalries, traumatic takeovers and ongoing battle between the creative people and those whose primary concern was profit and loss.

Rosie had heard most of the stories before and had some of her own to contribute. But much of the time she sat quietly listening, admiring the professional skill with which Nick was steering the conversation so that the funny stories were interspersed with more serious insights and the whole would, if videoed, have made a riveting chat-show.

As she had told Carolyn the night before, they had both been trained to bring other people out of sometimes unpromising shells. But Nick had a special flair for it. The reason Carolyn herself was in such sparkling form tonight was largely because he was feeding her all the right cues, giving her, while she was talking, the whole of his attention.

Tomorrow night they would be here on their own; an attractive amorous man and a pretty willing woman. The outcome seemed almost a foregone conclusion, unless Nick had the sense to see that a temporary liaison with his editor would be highly unwise. A serious involvement was another matter, but then it would be Marie-Laure he would have to ditch, and she might be deeply in love with him and not wish to be discarded.

The telephone rang.

'Excuse me.' Nick rose and crossed the room to answer it. *'Digame.'* A pause. 'Yes, she's here. Hold on a moment. It's for you, Carolyn . . . your brother.' He waited for her to come and take the receiver.

Guessing that her brother would not have telephoned her in Spain unless something untoward had happened, the others did not resume their conversation but watched Carolyn's expression becoming more and more worried as she listened to what her brother was saying.

'I shall have to make some enquiries. I'll ring you back. No, you'd better ring me again in about half an hour.'

She returned to the fireside, her face, so happy and animated a few minutes ago, now deeply worried.

'My father has been taken ill...a serious heart attack. I must get back as soon as possible. My mother needs me. She's not well herself and my brother can't go to her. He's due to fly to America early tomorrow and if he doesn't go it may jeopardise his job. How soon can I get back, Nick?'

'Not tonight, that's for sure. There may be a seat on a scheduled flight from Valencia or Alicante tomorrow morning. I'll find out.'

He strode away to his study.

'Have you no other relations or friends who can support your mother until you get back?' Rosie asked sympathetically.

'She does have a neighbour with her, but it's not the same,' said Carolyn. 'She and Dad were both only children so we don't have a lot of relations and Mother and my sister-in-law don't get on too well. Even if they did, Louise couldn't go to her. She has two-year-old twins to look after and she and Bob live in the North. My parents have retired to Dorset.' Looking ready to burst into tears, she wailed, 'Oh, why did this have to happen *now*...of all times?'

It was about twenty minutes before Nick returned, the line of his dark eyebrows indicating that he had nothing good to report.

'It looks as if the first flight you're likely to get on is the one the others are going back on. I'll make some more enquiries first thing in the morning but it doesn't look hopeful.'

During his absence it had become clear to Anna and Rosie that what Carolyn minded most was having her visit to Spain curtailed before there had been time to work on the book with Nick. Apparently she did not have the loving relationship with her parents that Rosie enjoyed and since her divorce, of which they had disapproved, had seen them only infrequently.

'Why not call your brother? Tell him you'll be there tomorrow evening and start going through your notes with Nick now. You're not going to sleep with this on your mind. I'm sure Nick won't mind burning some midnight oil,' Anna suggested.

He, not realising that it wasn't anxiety about her parents which was the chief weight on Carolyn's mind, said, 'Good lord, Anna, you can't expect Carolyn to put her mind to the book in these upsetting circumstances.' He patted Carolyn's shoulder. 'If you like I'll have a word with your brother and explain the situation. Then you can speak to your mother and tell her you'll definitely be with her tomorrow although you can't say what time you'll arrive.'

'But Bob's going to ring me back. I don't want to make long-distance calls at your expense,' she protested.

'My dear girl, my house is yours. You can ring again in the morning when you do know what time you'll arrive. Come and do it in my workroom where you can talk in private.' Taking her by the hand, he led her away.

'Very supportive, isn't he?' said Anna, when the jib-door had closed. 'Poor Carolyn. It is rotten luck for this to happen at a crucial point in the greatest coup of her career. Actually, from what she's told me, there's practically no editorial work to be done on the book. It really only needs line-editing. If she leaves her notes with Nick, they can probably sort out the few minor changes necessary by telephone.'

She yawned and stretched. 'I think the best thing you and I can do is to go to bed. Nick's is by far the best shoulder for her to cry on.'

'Sasha's in, but busy in the darkroom,' said Clare, when Rosie arrived home the next afternoon. 'How was Spain?'

Rosie gave her a potted report of the trip. It seemed far longer than three days since she had packed her case. She wished she had not gone, had refused to take on the promotion. Nick had occupied her mind all the way home, on the flight, on the train from Gatwick to Victoria, in the taxi to Fulham.

Even tomorrow, when she was back at work, she knew she was going to have a problem excluding him from her thoughts. The unpalatable fact was that during the short time she had spent at Font Vella, and in spite of all the common-sense arguments against it, she had relapsed; she was now as much in love with him as she had been before.

Inevitably Sasha, when she emerged from the darkroom, wanted to hear all about Nick and his place in Spain.

'It sounds a perfect background for a feature for *Hello!*. I'll call him this evening and see how soon we can set it up. What's his number?'

But when she dialled the monastery, it was a recording which answered and invited her to leave a message.

He was probably spending the evening at the bedside of Marie-Laure, thought Rosie.

He had insisted on driving them to the airport in case of any last hitches and when they had arrived at London a driver with Carolyn's surname written on a placard had been waiting to take her to Dorset. By now she should have been to see her father in the intensive care unit and be at her mother's number. Rosie felt it was only polite, having just spent the best part of three days in Carolyn's company, to telephone Dorset to enquire about her father.

'His condition is stable. They're not committing themselves about whether he'll pull through,' Carolyn told her, a few minutes later. 'Wasn't it thoughtful of Nick to organise a car for me...and pay for it, too? I only had to give the man a tip. I'd only been here a short time when Nick rang up to check that I had arrived. He said it could have been dangerous for me to drive myself here with my mind in a tizz about Father. He's going to ring again tomorrow. Talk about the antithesis of my ex, who never gave a thought to anyone's well-being but his own...'

Rosie knew it was stupid to be piqued because he had not telephoned to enquire if she had got home all right. He would take that for granted. Taught by her granny, who had lived at the farm during her widowhood and been a strong influence on Rosie until she was thirteen, that it was essential to write a letter of thanks after enjoying hospitality, after supper she went upstairs to the desk in her room to compose a short note of thanks.

Dear Nick,
    Our visit to Spain was most enjoyable, par-

ticularly at this time of year when the sun rarely shines in England. You have made El Monasterio into a beautiful house and I applaud your plan to do everything you can to keep Font Vella as unspoilt as it is at present.

I shall be writing to you shortly about the promotional plans for *Crusade* and should like to take this opportunity, in my private persona, of wishing you every success with it.

Thank you again for making us extremely comfortable and giving us a very pleasant break from routine. I'm sure everyone who comes to your corner of Spain in connection with the launch of *Crusade* will enjoy it as much as we did.

Best wishes.

Sincerely,
Rosie.

She was in bed, reading, when a soft tap on the door made her put down her book and call, 'Come in.'

It was a few minutes past eleven; after midnight in Spain. Several times the words she was reading had stopped making sense and she had had to drag her mind back from Font Vella to Fulham.

Sasha came in. 'Nick just called. We haven't fixed a date for me to go down there. He says there's no rush. It would be better to leave it till later in the year when the garden is at its best. I find it hard to see him as a keen gardener. Tom, yes. Not Nick.'

Sasha and Tom had split up because the summit of Tom's ambition was to become the editor of the *News*. With that object he had changed from reporting to sub-editing, that being the traditional route to top jobs on provincial newspapers.

Sasha had known she would never make chief photographer even if she'd wanted to. That post, on the *News* if not everywhere, was going to remain a male preserve for a long time to come.

Tom had wanted her to marry him and work part-time. She had loved him but been determined to make the most of her professional skills before settling down. After a volcanic row they had broken off their relationship, he to stay put, she to move to another newspaper before setting up as a freelance. Tom had found someone else and married her. Sasha had had several boyfriends but had never been seriously in love again.

'Funny: talking to Nick took me right back to the old *News* days,' she said. 'Seems a long time ago, doesn't it? We'll be thirty before we know it.'

'I expect we'll survive it. Other people do,' said Rosie.

She wondered if Sasha was thinking what she was thinking: that in spite of all they had achieved and their comfortable lifestyle, she could not truthfully claim to be completely happy, and she didn't think Sasha could either.

CHAPTER SEVEN

'YOU'RE a great gal, Rosie, you know that? It's been a whole lot of fun. We must do it again real soon. So long for now. Take care.'

With a final wave of the hand, the American science fiction writer disappeared into his hotel and Rosie got back into the taxi which had brought them from Heathrow and asked the driver to take her on to Fulham.

Being called a great gal recalled another American applying that description to someone else. It was not a welcome reminder. Three weeks had gone by since the visit to Spain. By now she had hoped to put it out of her mind. But, although she had been busy with other projects, she still felt unsettled.

Today had been long and tiring, which was why she had declined the writer's invitation to go up to his suite for a drink with his third wife, a compulsive shopper. All week his wife had been scouring London's department stores and boutiques while Rosie took the writer on tour to promote his latest book. It had already been on the *New York Times* bestseller list for twenty-three weeks and seemed likely to do equally well in Britain.

Today, through no fault of Rosie's, things had not gone smoothly. The writer had started the day with a hangover from a party last night. He had risen late, causing them almost to miss their shuttle flight to Manchester.

From there, after several radio and press interviews, they had been driven to Liverpool by a man with a heavy cold which he had done his best to share with them, sneezing and coughing all the way from the first city to the second. After the interviews in Liverpool, they had arrived at the airport to find the bar had just closed in the internal flights lounge and, worse, their take-off was delayed.

Fortunately experience had taught Rosie never to travel without a hip flask, not for her own use—although she had been known to add a reviving slug of gin to a glass of fruit juice after many hours in the company of a difficult client—but for the celebrities in her charge. By the end of a day which might have included a dozen or more interviews, they were usually in urgent need of a pick-me-up.

Aspirins, sticking plaster, throat lozenges, tablets to soothe nervous indigestion, chocolate for people whose energy flagged if they missed meals, hairspray, safety pins, a spare pair of one-size tights; these were only some of the things she had learnt to carry in her capacious tote-bag.

In general she didn't mind touring. Some PR consultants, once they were head of an agency or in a senior position, stopped going on the road, delegating all tours to their assistants except those involving the top-rank celebrities.

But Rosie had always liked touring and had refined and perfected the techniques involved so that maximum publicity was achieved with a minimum of nervous stress. It was one of the reasons why her agency had the edge on most of the others.

One of the most famous people she had ever escorted on a tour had said to her afterwards, 'Rosie, in a world where last-minute panics and carelessness are the norm, you are that rare thing, a perfectionist. You have anticipated every contingency. I have never been looked after better.'

But although, today, she had done what she could to reduce the annoyance of being stuck in a dry lounge for an hour and a half after the flight should have taken off, and the writer been pleased to be plied with gin, he had not wanted to relax with the copy of *Time* she had offered him.

Despite having done nothing else all week, he had wanted to talk about himself and had done so throughout their wait, in flight and between the airport and his hotel. There was nothing about his antecedents, his youth, his wives, his children, his health, his emotional problems that he had left untold. Had she taken it all down in shorthand, Rosie could have written his biography.

'What was the number, miss?' the driver asked, as the taxi turned into her street.

'Twenty-three . . . on the right. Where the bollards are holding the parking space.'

The presence of the plastic bollards meant that Sasha was not yet back from her trip to Brighton to photograph a well-known actor and his wife at home.

Looking forward to a long soak in the jacuzzi followed by a light supper and quiet evening alone in her room, Rosie paid the fare and climbed the steps to the front door, latch-key in hand.

She had closed the door behind her and was starting to mount the stairs when a sound from the direction of the kitchen brought a puzzled frown to her face. What she had heard had been laughter—a man's laughter.

What was a man doing here? The only time men entered the house was when they gave one of their parties or when, occasionally, it was necessary to have some repair done.

The sound of laughter came again. This time Clare was laughing as well. Intrigued, Rosie put down her tote-bag and went to investigate.

In the kitchen she found her housekeeper sitting at the table peeling sprouts with a glass of sherry beside the bowl in which she was dropping the discarded leaves.

Nearby, leaning against the dresser, forearms crossed, amusement at whatever had made them laugh still lingering on his tanned face, was Nick Winchester.

At the sight of Rosie he straightened and unfolded his arms.

'Rosie... hello. How are you?'

He came round the end of the table, placed both hands on her shoulders and bent his tall head to brush a light kiss on her left cheek and then her right cheek.

It was, as she had observed in the village restaurant and again at his drinks party, the custom in Spain for people to kiss on meeting.

But, already taken aback by Nick's unexpected presence in her house, she was even more startled by this affectionate greeting.

'What are you doing here?' she exclaimed.

'I'm in London for a few days and I thought I would look you up and say hello to Sasha.'

'You've had a long day, Rosie. Sit down and have a glass of this super sherry Mr Winchester has brought,' said Clare, rising to fetch a glass from the dresser.

Although he no longer had his hands on her shoulders, Nick was still standing disturbingly close. Rosie was glad to move away and sink on to the comfortable old sofa, re-covered with red and white ticking, which helped to give the kitchen its homely air.

'What time did you arrive?' she asked. For, although Clare had called him Mr Winchester, they had both looked very much at ease when she joined them.

'About an hour ago, I guess. Clare said she was expecting both of you back about now so I stuck around. You don't mind, I hope?'

'Not at all,' she said politely.

Nick filled the glass with sherry and brought it to her. 'I hear you've been on tour with the sci-fi writer whose book I saw advertised all the way up an Underground escalator today. What's he like?'

'In print he's great—if you like reading sci-fi. In private . . . rather a pain,' said Rosie, kicking off her shoes and tucking her legs up beside her.

Nick seated himself at the other end of the sofa, which fortunately was a long one so there was a space between them.

'I hope I don't merit that judgement after our tour. The main reason I came over was for a final run-through the book with Carolyn. Now I'm at a loose end until my flight back tomorrow.'

'If Carolyn knew you were coming, I'm surprised she hasn't made arrangements to entertain you.'

'We've already had lunch together two days running. I'm sure she has had more than enough of my company for the time being,' he said smoothly.

I'll bet she hasn't, thought Rosie. What you mean is that you didn't want to see more of her.

'Did you see Anna while you were at the office?' she asked.

He shook his head. 'I didn't go to the office. We worked at Carolyn's flat. She said if we worked at B & P there would be constant interruptions.'

'How is her father?'

'Better . . . making good progress. I was hoping you and Sasha would take pity on an out-of-towner and have dinner with me.'

'I can't speak for Sasha, but to be honest I'm bushed. I've been running around all week. Tonight I'd like to relax.'

'Sasha's had a busy week too. If Mr Winchester doesn't mind simple home cooking, there's more than enough for the three of you,' Clare said quietly.

The remark made it difficult for Rosie not to invite him to supper. It surprised and annoyed her that Clare should put her in that position. Usually Clare was careful to make it clear to their visitors that Rosie and Sasha owned the house and she was an employee.

Rosie said, 'I should think, as you lead a quiet life in Spain, you're looking forward to a night on the town. Sasha may be delighted to live it up with you. She's probably had an easier day than I have.'

'Perhaps, but I expect she'd still rather relax at home. So would I, if you'll let me?'

There was nothing to do but give in gracefully. 'Of course.' She drained her glass. 'But you'll have to excuse me for half an hour. I'm going to take a bath.'

A short time later, up to her chin in the scented foam of the French bubble gel she reserved as a special treat when life was more than usually taxing, she heard

Clare enter the bedroom to take away her shoes and clothes.

'Clare, would you come in a minute?' she called.

The older woman appeared in the doorway. She was wearing a red dress which Rosie had seen before without being struck, as she was now, by how well the colour set off Clare's colouring. She was dark, with a streak of white hair springing from the left side of her broad forehead.

'Clare, I could have done without a guest this evening. What made you invite Nick to wait for us to come home? It would have been better to suggest that he rang up later.'

'I suppose it would, but he seemed at a loose end and, to be honest, *I* wanted to meet him,' said Clare. 'I've often seen him and liked him on television. I was glad of the chance to talk to him. I get a bit lonely sometimes, on my own here all day. But that's no excuse. I'm sorry, Rosie.'

The humility of her apology made Rosie feel mean to have remonstrated with her.

'I'm sorry too. I shouldn't have taken my tiredness out on you. I'm feeling antisocial tonight.'

'But he's not like the man you've been looking after this week. He's nice...he's fun...he'll make you laugh,' said Clare. 'I thought you were old friends from way back. That's the impression he gave me.'

'Did he? Well, he exaggerated. We were never close friends, just colleagues in the same office. And I shouldn't think for a moment that he's really at a loose end. He must know scores of people in London. I can't imagine why he should pick on me and Sasha to descend on.'

'As you stayed at his place in Spain not long ago, isn't it possible he wanted to see you again...that he's attracted to you?' Clare suggested.

It was a possibility which had crossed Rosie's mind, to be immediately dismissed as a piece of dangerous self-delusion.

Wishful thinking about men was, she knew, a weakness of her sex. In her own circle of acquaintance, there were women who had wasted years of their lives on the patently false hope that some guy would come up to scratch, either by falling in love with them, or leaving his wife for them, or keeping his promise not to cheat on them, or whatever it might be that would make them happy.

'If Nick were in the market for a wife, I think he'd have found one by now, Clare,' she answered drily.

'Not necessarily. The right person can be hard to find...for both sexes,' Clare answered, equally drily. 'I'm thirty-eight and I haven't met the right man yet...and probably never will now,' she added.

She turned and walked out of the bathroom, leaving Rosie to wonder, yet again, what had gone wrong between her and Angie's father. Clare would have made him such a wonderful wife, but perhaps he had been too young to want one.

She had changed into flannel trousers and a paler grey cashmere sweater with moderate shoulder-pads, with a belt of ochre punched suede slotted through the loops of the trousers and large yellow amber earrings, when she heard Sasha coming in.

Evidently Nick was in the living-room because Sasha's shout of surprise at finding him there could be heard in the room above.

Presently she heard her friend running upstairs and then tapping on the bathroom door. Although it adjoined Rosie's bedroom, it also had a door to the landing, as did the shower-room linked to Sasha's bedroom.

She heard Sasha call, 'Are you still wallowing, Rosie?'

Opening her bedroom door, Rosie said, 'No, I'm here,' and beckoned Sasha in. 'How did Brighton go?'

'Terrific...a breeze. They gave me a super lunch and it all went to plan. Hey, what a surprise to find Nick here!'

'Yes, and as far as I'm concerned not a particularly welcome one. My day was hell on wheels and I'd promised myself a relaxing evening.'

'What are you fussing about? Your hair's not a mess. You don't look bushed. You look great.'

'Sasha, that isn't the point. How I look is irrelevant. I wanted a quiet evening.'

'So have one. Let Nick do the talking. If you can't be bothered to sparkle, maybe I will. I quite fancy him now, as a matter of fact. If you're really not interested, it might be amusing to divert his interest to me. If I can, that is.'

'I should think any passable female could divert him...temporarily. But when you go down to Spain to do the feature on him, you'll find his longer-term needs are catered for by a Frenchwoman—possibly a widow but more likely a divorcée—who lives in the same village.'

'Really? Did you meet her?'

'No, but I heard about her and she's in his book. Before you start something with him, you'd better read it. He's obviously found himself one of those legendary Frenchwomen who cooks, dresses, decorates her house, entertains and makes love about ten times better than the rest of us.'

'If she's as wonderful as that, why doesn't he snap her up?'

'I've no idea. Maybe she doesn't want to be snapped up. Maybe she's had a husband and finds a lover better. That could be the essence of her charm . . . that she makes no demands. Anyway, be warned. Tangling with Nick could end in tears.'

'I'll bear it in mind,' said Sasha. 'Right now I'm going to take a quick tub. I've been looking forward to it all the way back from Brighton.'

When Rosie went downstairs, aware that her strictures to Sasha had an element of hypocrisy in them because if Nick hadn't been here she would have worn jeans and a sweatshirt and not bothered to replace her make-up after taking it off for her bath, she found him reading a copy of the Brighton newspaper Sasha had brought back.

'Not bad . . . not as good as the *News*, although I dare say that's changed a good deal since our time,' he said, as she joined him. 'Do you ever miss journalism, Rosie?'

'Not really. I'm still in contact with journalists, national and provincial. Magazine people too. I have the best of all worlds.'

'You two have certainly made yourselves very comfortable here . . . and what a nice woman Clare is.'

'Yes, we're very lucky to have her.'

'When she mentioned having a daughter, I would have assumed she was a widow or separated, but she's neither, I gather. Whoever left her in the lurch must be a bit of a bastard.'

'Perhaps not ... just young and feckless. He may not even have known she was pregnant. She never talks about it.'

'Obviously you and Sasha don't want to lose her, but it seems sad for her to go through life on her own.'

'I think Clare's quite content. Marriage isn't always all it's cracked up to be.'

'No, but when it does work it's a good way to live. You don't plan to be wedded to your career forever, do you?'

'Having got this far, I don't plan to give it up... which is what marriage might demand. Sasha and I are in much the same position as you are. We've organised a life for ourselves in which our only need for a man is as a lover.'

'And to father your children ... or have children no place in your scheme of things?'

They had, but she wasn't going to tell him that. Having enjoyed being part of a large family herself, she had always included three or four children as part of her life-plan.

She shrugged. 'Do they have a place in yours?'

To her surprise, he said, 'Yes. At the time I bought the monastery, I wasn't thinking of it in terms of an ideal house for a large family. But now I should very much like to fill it with my progeny. Being an only child myself, I've always envied people like you who grew up with brothers and sisters to play with.'

'You surprise me. Although obviously you enjoy pleasant and comfortable surroundings, I shouldn't have suspected you of wanting to be a paterfamilias.'

'I'm equally surprised to find you a dedicated career woman.'

'I don't like that expression. It makes the women it's applied to sound strange and unnatural. No one regards it as strange for a man to take his job seriously and give it most of his attention. Why should it be considered odd in a woman?'

'You're right, of course, but a moment ago you found it odd of me to want to have five or six kids running around the monastery. Why should it be thought normal for your sex to want children but peculiar when men do?'

Sasha came down the stairs. Usually for evenings at home, she wore a velour tracksuit. Tonight she had changed into a flame-coloured chenille sweater with a long string of red Chinese beads and a very short black leather skirt with her sexiest black diamond-pattern tights.

'Haven't you offered him a drink yet, Rosie? He must be longing for one. What would you like, Nick?'

It was, for Rosie, a strange evening, superficially relaxed and convivial but with an underlying tension.

She could see that the two other women took to Nick unreservedly. And indeed he was very good company, never holding the floor for too long, as interested in them as they were in him.

It seemed to Rosie that, in spite of her warning, Sasha was exerting herself to charm him.

After they had eaten and Clare had tactfully withdrawn to her own quarters, Sasha said, 'If you've nothing better to do tomorrow, would you like to come with me? I've got a short job in Reading—it won't take more than an hour—and I know a pub in the area where they do a very good lunch; I could drop you at Heathrow in time for your flight.'

'That would be fine. Why don't you come too, Rosie?'

'Too busy, I'm afraid.' Had he really wanted to include her, or had that been merely politeness?

'Pity: some country air—if Berkshire counts as the country—would have done you good. Have you had a cold since you came to Spain? You look a bit wan.'

She shook her head. 'I feel fine. Most people here are pale at this time of year, unless they've been lying in the sun somewhere.'

'Sasha always was pale. It's her colouring. But you used to have rosy cheeks. Rosie by name, and rosy by nature, you were.'

'Roly-poly and rosy...sounds like a pink pork sausage. Which was rather what I used to look like. Thank God I don't any more. What you call wan, others call pale and interesting. I've got some papers to look through before tomorrow, so I'm going to say goodnight...and goodbye.'

She stood up and held out her hand and Nick rose and kissed it, not just bowing and brushing it lightly but pressing a proper kiss on the back of her palm.

She could still feel the warmth of his lips on her hand when she reached her room. She sank on to the bed and then lay back on the duvet and, hardly knowing what she was doing, laid the back of her hand on her mouth as if, by so doing, she could somehow transfer the feel of his lips to hers.

I want him, she thought. I want to know what it's like to be in his arms, to hold him in my arms. But I don't know if he wants me. He seems more interested in Sasha now. Oh, God, I can't bear it if they have an affair. It's bad enough that he's involved with the Frenchwoman. But to have him coming here often, perhaps spending nights with Sasha—that would be unbearable. We discussed what to do about lovers before we bought the house; we agreed that there might be occasions when we might want a man to spend the night with us and, handled with discretion, that would be all right. And it was. When Sasha was involved with Miles, he slept with her under this roof and nobody minded. Both Clare and I turned a blind eye. It was Sasha's business.

But if it were Nick it would be different. I couldn't ignore his presence in Sasha's bed. It would be torture.

I love him, damn him. I love him. I always have, and I know now that I always will.

CHAPTER EIGHT

ROSIE'S lunch at her desk the next day was a pot of low-fat yoghurt and an orange.

Now, every time she ate an orange, it would remind her of the fruit Nick had picked for her breakfast at El Monasterio. An imported orange did not have the same essence-of-sunlight flavour as one plucked from a tree.

She thought of Sasha and Nick, holed up in some cosy pub, a free house with real oak beams and real horse-brasses and a landlord who had resisted the pressure to install a juke-box.

She could have been eating with them, tucking into home-made steak and kidney pudding, or shepherd's pie, or Cheddar cheese and pickled onions, instead of being here by herself, eating yoghurt with a teaspoon to make it last as long as possible.

She felt a wave of nostalgia for the farm and Mum's hearty home cooking and the days when the only people she had loved had been her family.

Now she loved Sasha as much, perhaps more than she loved her married sisters whom she saw only once or twice a year, at Christmas and during a weekend at home in the summer. And, against her will, she loved Nick.

How could she bear it if Sasha turned out to be the right woman for him? Sasha's career was portable. A freelance photo-journalist had to be mobile, but her base could be anywhere.

Whether Sasha would be prepared to have a large family Rosie wasn't sure. It was not something they had discussed. Almost everything else, but not that.

Like Nick, her friend had neither brothers nor sisters. It was not impossible that she might have a latent desire to make up for being an 'only' by having lots of children herself.

At this very moment something might be starting between her and Nick which would ultimately lead to the Frenchwoman's leaving Font Vella and Sasha's leaving Fulham.

The thought of it wrenched Rosie's insides. It was bad enough being in love with a man who had an irresistibly charming mistress. It would be far worse if he fell for her best friend and settled down to make her an ideal husband.

For, deep down, Rosie felt sure that Nick had it in him to be a marvellous husband. Once he found the right woman.

Perhaps what had stopped him from marrying Marie-Laure was that she was a few years older than he was, too old to bear the children he wanted. Yet, if he loved her, would he care about that?

A woman might have such a powerful maternal instinct that not having children could blight her life, but surely a man's wish to father children was never as strong as his desire for a woman he wanted?

If Nick truly loved Marie-Laure it would not matter to him that she was past or nearly past child-bearing age. Love did not demand that the loved one should be perfect in every way. Love didn't ask to be given; it wanted to give, to unload all life's best gifts on the beloved, regardless of self.

Maybe it was for that reason that Marie-Laure, having been asked, had refused to marry him. She might long to be his wife but feel that happiness was barred to her because she could never give him the large family he wanted.

Forcing herself to concentrate on the job in hand, checking a list of women's page editors who were to be sent review copies of a new book on knitting, Rosie found two omissions.

When the most junior of her four assistants came back from her lunch break, Rosie called her into her office.

'You've been working here for three months now, Judy, and it's time we could rely on you to do things without somebody having to check them for careless slips. Yesterday I noticed you leaving ten minutes early and you're often late in the mornings. I know buses don't always run on schedule but at this stage of your career—if you're serious about it—you should be prepared to get up early enough to be here on time no matter what.'

'I'm sorry.' Judy hung her head and bit her lip. She was the brightest and best of the applicants for her job, but clearly she felt that life began at five-thirty and that Rosie was a pernickety fusspot whom it was impossible to satisfy.

'I'm sorry too, because this agency has been built on hard work and dedicated efficiency, and, the next time you fail to check and double-check that the job you've done is perfect, I'm afraid I'll have to ask you to leave. We just don't have room for a passenger. Now take this list away and correct it, please.'

At the end of the working day, Rosie stayed at her desk because later she was going to a party at the Royal

Automobile Club to launch a catalogue sponsored by the Booksellers' Association.

The two juniors had already gone when her senior assistant came in with two mugs of decaff and said, 'I found Judy in tears in the loo this afternoon. You threatened her with the sack, I gather.'

Rosie nodded. 'If we've got to check everything she does, we might as well do it ourselves. When I made careless mistakes in my copy after three months as a junior reporter, I got a blast from the chief sub which would have made a midshipman in Nelson's Navy cringe.'

Even as she said it, Rosie realised that it was the kind of remark which, when older people said something similar, made her think, Oh, lord, here we go, back to the good old days when everything was so much better than now.

'Am I beginning to sound like a dragon?' she asked.

Her colleague shook her head. 'There's nothing like a little fire and brimstone for gingering up juniors. We may have to give her the push anyway. If a stern word from you is enough to reduce her to sobs in the loo, how will she ever cope with escorting a difficult author round the Birmingham-Wolverhampton circuit?'

Reminded of one of her own first tours, Rosie laughed.

She and a woman writer, who was equally inexperienced, had set out by train for the Midlands. The author had dressed for a major chat-show on TV rather than question-and-answer sessions with local radio presenters interspersed with Press interviews, one of which had taken place in the newspaper's crowded front office, another in an even more crowded pub.

The schedule had not allowed enough time for lunch. They had had to make do with cheese rolls in a station buffet and the writer, whose feet were hurting after rushing around on stilettoes, had plumped down on a seat which had had a dollop of ketchup spilt on it.

Nowadays Rosie sent all her clients a copy of 'Twenty tips for trouble-free touring', a leaflet of her own devising which she knew had been pirated by at least one other agency.

Reassured that she had not been unduly harsh with Judy and in a more cheerful mood, Rosie went on working until it was time to go to the party. Then she changed her sweater for a silk shirt, replaced the gold hoops in her ears with large silver tassels and her neat black loafers with pumps and set off determined to enjoy herself.

An hour later a literary agent invited her to join a group having supper at the Groucho Club.

It was late when she got back to Fulham but the light was on in the kitchen and an inviting aroma was wafting up to the hall. Clare must have been having one of her evening cookery sessions. She went down to speak to her.

'Hello, Rosie.' Their housekeeper was tidying up, her face flushed from the extra warmth generated by having several hobs and the oven on. 'Sasha's in the darkroom, developing the film she used today. Have you eaten?'

'Yes, thanks. What have you been making?'

'Fruit bread . . . a couple of casseroles . . . things for the freezer. Look what came for me this morning. Aren't they lovely?' She pointed to the large bunch of daffodils—at least six ordinary bunches combined—massed in a tall square glass vase at the cooler end of the kitchen.

'They're from Nick. There's a big bunch of narcissi upstairs for you and Sasha. Wasn't it thoughtful of him to thank the cook as well as his hostesses?'

'Very.'

'And a note as well...look.' Clare took from the dresser a florist's card and handed it to her.

Nick had written, 'Alice B. Toklas said that many first-rate women cooks had tired eyes and a wan smile, but clearly there are notable exceptions. Thank you for an excellent dinner and for making me welcome in your kitchen. N.W.'

'Who was Alice B. Toklas?' asked Clare. 'The name rings a bell but I can't place her.'

'You've probably noticed her cookery book somewhere. She and Gertrude Stein were Americans who lived in Paris between the wars and earlier. Gertrude Stein was a writer and a friend of artists like Picasso and Braque. She and Alice were, in effect, married.'

'You make me feel dreadfully ill-read,' said Clare.

'You and Angie make me feel horribly ignorant about music,' Rosie answered. 'We can't all be knowledgeable about everything.'

'I shouldn't think there are many subjects on which Nick isn't well-informed. Some of the famous people you and Sasha have asked to your parties have been no end of a disappointment to me. But he isn't. I could listen to him talking all night. I suppose he'll be back in Spain now.'

'Probably. I'm going to bed. Goodnight, Clare.'

On her way up to her room, she paused to inhale the light scent of the narcissi which must have brought their promise of spring from the Scilly Isles. It was too early for them to be out on the mainland.

The message on the card propped against the vase was, 'My thanks to you both for a most enjoyable evening. Nick.'

When Rosie reached the landing, the warning light was on outside the darkroom. She would not hear about Sasha's lunch with Nick until tomorrow.

Sasha came down to breakfast with a folder in her hand.

'What do you think of these?' She opened the folder and handed Rosie a six-by-eight black and white print of Nick leaning over a field gate.

That he was photogenic had already been proved on TV. The camera, unflattering to some faces, was not to his. The print reproduced his strong features and the brilliance of his eyes with the same charismatic effect they had when one met him. The quizzical lift of the eyebrow, the wide, amused mouth— the charm of the man was all there. Rosie's heart flipped over like a deftly tossed pancake.

'I took twenty-four and they've all come out well,' said Sasha. 'He's a natural. Couldn't care less what he looks like. Most men would have combed their hair and gone all stiff and self-conscious. He just did what I asked, like a pro, but without any preening.'

She handed Rosie shot after shot of Nick rambling around the countryside in the same corduroy jeans and chunky sweater over a cotton shirt he had worn the night before last. But in the photographs, the day being cold, the sweater was topped by a well-worn flier's-style jacket. The leather had moulded itself to the shape of his powerful shoulders.

'Did he ask you to take them?' Rosie asked.

'No, but he mentioned over lunch that Bury & Poole wanted to organise a shoot with a top photographer which Nick thought was rather a bore. So I said, Let me have a go. I think one of those should be OK for the back of his book, don't you?'

'They're excellent, but B & P will probably want a colour transparency.'

'I have a whole roll of them.'

'Did you get him to the airport on time?'

'Of course. Did you think I wouldn't?'

'No, but you hadn't been planning to do these.'

'It didn't take long. I'm probably going to Spain at the end of May or early in June. I can't wait to see his house.'

To see the house, or to see him again? Rosie wondered, with a pang.

Spring came. Rosie threw herself into an orgy of work, taking on commitments which meant that she had to work late at night and most weekends.

By this means she managed, for quite long stretches of time, to convince herself that nothing was wrong with her life. But it was like papering over a crack in a wall. Every so often the paper began to split, the crack to reappear.

This happened on days when the fax machine transmitted a letter from Spain concerning the drafts of the various Press releases they would be sending out about *Crusade*.

It happened when Nick telephoned her.

It happened when his name came up in conversations with Anna or the other people involved in launching his book.

Bury & Poole had their own paperback imprint and by now it had been decided to bring *Crusade* out as what was known as a 'trade' paperback. This meant it would be published in hardback for sale to libraries and people who could afford the high price of hardbacks. But the big sales would come from an extra-large paperback sold at half the price of the hardback, although not as cheaply as the 'mass market' standard-size paperback which would follow it a year later.

Bury & Poole had a very livewire marketing manager called Sherry and had recently taken on an equally sparky promotions manager called Janetta. Both Sherry and Janetta had been invited to El Monasterio and had come back with redoubled enthusiasm.

Whenever Rosie was in contact with them about other titles on their list, invariably they had something to say about Nick. Both were fairly recently married so they hadn't fallen for him, but, as Sherry remarked, 'It gives one's enthusiasm an extra edge when the author is such a dish.'

They had not, it seemed, met Marie-Laure. Evidently Nick didn't believe in mixing business with pleasure and did not plan to introduce the women who were in his life in connection with *Crusade* to the woman who beguiled his leisure hours.

One evening when, as was usual now, she was working late, the telephone chirped and Nick's voice, instantly recognisable, said, 'I called you at home but Clare said you'd be at your desk. She thinks you're overworking.'

'Nonsense—I thrive on hard work.' Her pulse had begun to race. 'What can I do for you?'

'When Sasha comes down, why don't you come with her? Not to talk promo... to relax and enjoy. A break in the sun would do you good. When did you last do nothing for a few days?'

'I went home for Christmas.'

'But was that relaxing, with all your nephews and nieces in full cry?'

'They didn't bother me. The men looked after the kids and took care of the washing-up and the women produced the meals and then lolled round the fire, eating chocs and chatting.'

Rosie herself had not succumbed to the chocolates, but she had allowed herself a few indulgences, including a slice of her mother's home-made Christmas pudding, always served with a sprig of holly stuck in the top and twelve emblems, wrapped in greaseproof paper, hidden inside it.

Her slice of pudding had contained the tiny silver thimble—an heirloom used by her father's great-grandmother as a small child learning to sew—which represented spinsterhood. Rosie had laughed and not minded because that was before she met Nick again, before being single forever had changed from a possibility to a probability.

'Christmas was five months ago, and a girl who works as hard as you do needs regular breaks. Why not come with Sasha?' he persisted.

And, because he sounded as if he really wanted her to come, for a few seconds she wavered and nearly agreed to go.

But then Nick added, 'I think Sasha would feel more comfortable having you with her. You can chaperon each other.'

Instantly Rosie perceived the real reason for his invitation. It was not for the pleasure of her company that he wanted her there but so that the presence of an attractive unaccompanied girl in his house should not cause gossip in the village and in the expatriate community.

Also he might think that having Sasha there by herself would not meet with Encarna's approval. It would certainly not please the Frenchwoman. No woman of mature years could be pleased at the presence of someone as stunning as Sasha in her lover's house. She would be as jealous as hell.

'Thanks very much...it's kind of you. But as a matter of fact I have a break planned for around the same time as Sasha is coming to Spain. I'm going on a bicycle tour of Normandy and Brittany,' Rosie said briskly, borrowing the holiday plans of the person she had lunched with that day.

'I see. That sounds fun. Are you going in a group?' he asked.

'No, with a friend.'

'Another girl?'

It was on the tip of her tongue to say yes. Then she changed her mind and said, 'No...with a man. But that's off the record. I'd rather the word wasn't spread on the book world grapevine. I like to keep my private life private.'

There was a slight pause before he said, 'Your secret is safe with me. I hope you have a good time. Well, that's all I called about, so I'll let you get back to whatever I interrupted. Bye bye, Rosie.'

Most of Sasha's luggage for her trip to Spain consisted of photographic equipment. Two swimsuits, an uncrushable evening outfit, one pair of shorts, a couple of T-shirts and the clothes she was wearing to travel was the extent of her wardrobe.

'Anything else I might need, I can buy when I get there,' she said, stuffing her personal gear into a roll-bag.

Since the night of Nick's telephone call and her fib about cycling through northern France with a male companion, Rosie had often wondered what had possessed her to lie to him.

As she didn't want him accidentally to find out that the trip had been a spur of the moment fabrication, she said to Sasha, 'Nick seemed to feel you ought to be chaperoned and cast me in that role. But I'm sure you can cope with any passes he may make at you, and I'm far too busy to take time off. So I made an excuse about going on a jaunt with Carl later in the month. If he asks, don't let on it was a white lie, will you?'

Sasha looked slightly puzzled but agreed not to. 'You haven't seen Carl for ages, have you?'

'I suppose it is quite some time. I must give him a buzz this week.' Rosie changed the subject.

Sasha's visit to Spain coincided with her car's need for a major service so she took it to the garage the day before she left and Rosie ran her to the airport. The roll-bag containing her friend's clothes would go in the hold with the tripod and other less precious equipment so that Sasha could take her cameras and lenses—one of which had cost more than a thousand pounds—in the cabin with her.

'Have a great time,' Rosie said, as they hugged goodbye.

'I will. See you next week. Bye, Rosie.'

Her dark eyes shining with pleasurable antici-pation—did they also have the extra sparkle of a woman on her way to meet a man in whom she had a special interest?—Sasha wheeled her laden luggage-trolley the direction of the check-in desks.

Everyone, seeing someone off on a journey to somewhere lovely, felt a bit depressed at being left out of the adventure, Rosie told herself as she drove back to London.

She began to wonder if it would be a good idea to go cycling with Carl.

Two days before Sasha was due back, Rosie returned from the office to be greeted by Clare with the news that her friend had changed her plans and would be staying in Spain for a second week.

'She sounded very excited and said something had come up and she needed at least another week there,' said Clare. 'I asked why and she laughed and said it was far too complicated to explain on the telephone. But I expect she didn't want to make an extended long-distance call on Nick's phone. You could give her a buzz if you're curious to find out what's happening.'

'I could but I don't think I will,' Rosie said lightly. 'We'll hear all about it in due course. I seem to spend my life on the telephone. I'm beginning to get PR consultant's shoulder.' She hitched her shoulder into the position needed to hold a receiver in place while using her hands for some other task. 'Also the tele-phone bills are really going through the roof. I must try to cut out some of the unnecessary calls, es-pecially the long-distance ones.'

Neither of these excuses was the real reason why she didn't want to call Sasha. She was acting on instinct, and instinct told her that whatever Sasha had to tell was not something she would want to hear.

It was the first time since they had set up house together that they had been apart for so long and, although she had Clare to talk to if she wanted companionship, Rosie missed Sasha even more than she had anticipated.

The week seemed to pass interminably slowly but at last the day of Sasha's return arrived. Before setting out to meet her, Rosie checked that the flight had left Spain and was due to arrive on time.

She had left her car in the short-term park and was among the crowd waiting behind the barrier outside the Customs hall when people with brown or lobster-red faces, dressed for a spring night in Benidorm, began to emerge from the hall.

Sasha was one of the last and, with her naturally dark colouring, she had acquired a beautiful deep, even tan. Rosie had never seen her look as glamorous, or as happy.

CHAPTER NINE

'Hı! How are you?'

As soon as she was clear of the barrier, Sasha gave Rosie a big hug and kissed her on both cheeks, Spanish fashion.

'I've got so much to tell . . . I don't know where to begin.'

'Let's get your gear in the car first,' Rosie suggested.

'No, we can't leave yet,' said Sasha. 'I'm afraid we're going to have to stick around for an hour.'

'What for?'

'I haven't come back alone. At least I have, but I haven't . . . if you see what I mean.' She was grinning from ear to ear.

'No, I don't.'

'Someone is with me but not on my flight. Rosie, you'll never guess what's happened in a million years. I can't believe it myself. Darling, sweet, adorable Nick——'

'Is also coming back,' Rosie interrupted her. 'What time is his flight due?' She felt as if someone had kicked her hard in the stomach.

'Not Nick. Why should he come back? It's Tom who's coming. You can't have forgotten Tom. He was there when I arrived at the monastery. Nick had invited him down. Look, I can't tell you all about it here. Let's go to the restaurant or somewhere.'

They managed to find a table for two in the cafeteria. Leaving Sasha to mind the luggage, Rosie

124

queued for a couple of beakers of airport coffee. She wasn't thirsty, but she needed a breathing space to get back on balance after the horrible shock she had just had.

She had foreseen it, of course, had been dreading it all this long week. Even so, it had hit her like a punch in the guts.

Now it seemed she had misunderstood. It wasn't Nick who was responsible for Sasha's radiance. It was Tom. But how could that be? Tom was married...had been married for ages.

However, as she discovered a few minutes later, Tom was not married after all. His engagement had been broken off and he was still a bachelor, although he would not remain in that state for long. He had applied for an editorship in Australia, had got the job and was leaving in a few weeks' time. Sasha was going with him, as his wife.

'We wanted to fly back together but it wasn't possible. He flew to Valencia because it's a city he's always wanted to see,' Sasha explained. 'Apparently he and Nick have always kept in touch. That day Nick and I had lunch, I admitted to Nick that Tom was the reason I've never got serious with anyone else. Suspecting that Tom felt the same way, although he had always denied it, Nick decided that, as I was coming to Font Vella anyway, he would try his hand at matchmaking.'

'And couldn't have been more successful. I'm very happy for you, Sasha. I shall miss you dreadfully, but——'

'You'll have to come and stay with us...and don't worry about replacing me as co-owner of the house because Nick has put up a scheme for that too.'

'You're not proposing to sell your share to him, are you?' Rosie exclaimed, aghast.

'I did suggest it,' said Sasha. 'I thought he might like to have *pied-à-terre* in London instead of having to stay at hotels. But he says he doesn't want a property here. If he had a flat anywhere it would be in New York. He wants to lend the money to Clare so that she can buy my share of the house. He thinks she's had a tough life and ought to have the security of being a house-owner, or at any rate a half-house-owner. Don't you think it's a good idea?'

'Yes, I do,' Rosie agreed. 'If I've got to lose you, there's no one I'd rather share with than Clare. But will she agree?'

'Why not? I think she'll jump at it. Anyway Nick is coming over for our wedding, which will be as soon as we can arrange it. You and Clare can discuss the house situation with him then.'

Having helped to drink the bottles of *cava* which Sasha and Tom had brought back to accompany the meal Clare had prepared for Sasha's homecoming, and which had easily stretched to become a celebration *à quatre*, Rosie did not lie awake when she went to bed that night.

But, having neglected to drink a glass or two of water last thing, she was woken up in the small hours by a terrible thirst. By the time she had crept downstairs to quench it with refrigerated spring water, and crept back to her room, she was wide awake, with much to keep her that way.

Her predominant emotion was relief that Sasha was in love with a man who had no other commitments to cast a blight on their happiness. An involvement with Nick would not only have been marred by his association with the Frenchwoman, but for Rosie, if not for Sasha, it would also have tarnished their friendship.

It was Tom who, some hours later when the three of them were having breakfast, said, 'Nick is bringing Marie-Laure over for our wedding. You haven't met her yet, have you, Rosie? Except in the sense that everyone who's read *Crusade* has met her?'

'She was in the clinic at Benidorm the weekend I was at Font Vella. So she *is* the model for Laure in Nick's book? I wondered about that.'

It was Sasha who said, 'There's no question about it. Laure is drawn straight from life . . . with one or two adjustments.'

Rosie swallowed the lump in her throat. 'I'll look forward to meeting her. Anyone who can inspire a character like Laure must be delightful.'

'She is . . . you'll adore her. I wanted to photograph her in her blissful little house but she wouldn't let me. She has this deep, sexy voice which sounds so odd coming from a person you feel might blow away in a strong gust of wind. "I much regret, Sasha darleeng, you 'ave come too late . . . far too late," she said to me. "I want to leave for posterity only the portraits painted of me in my prime. At fiftee, even at sixtee, I was not bad . . . but soon I must veil all the mirrors so as not to catch even a glimpse of what time 'as done to me."'

'In fact she's a knockout still,' Tom said, smiling.

'But how old is she?' Rosie demanded.

'Oh, eighty at least, I should think. Possibly more. But as sharp as a razor mentally . . . and funny! She has you in fits.'

'I thought ... I had the impression she was Nick's mistress.'

The other two roared with laughter.

'I should think she probably would be if she were younger,' said Sasha. 'She adores him and he her. I have actually seen her watching him with a rather wistful look in her eyes, as if she were wishing they hadn't been born about forty-five years out of sync. It's a good thing she is an old lady. I've seen a portrait of her, painted in 1960, and, believe me, she was *ravishing*. Had she still been fiftyish, I shouldn't have stood a chance. Nick and Tom would have been fighting over her.'

'Not I,' Tom told her fondly. 'But she would have suited Nick. They're two of a kind. It's too bad he can't find someone to share that great house with him, and all the money he's going to make from the book.'

There was a pause. Aware that Sasha was looking at her, Rosie concentrated on picking up pieces of shell peeled from the top of her boiled egg and dropping them tidily inside the intact shell.

Then Tom said, 'Do you think he's interested in Clare? She seems very nice, and this plan to lend her the money to buy you out does suggest that he might be.'

Clare was not in the house. Normally she did have breakfast with them but today, with her usual tact, she had breakfasted early and now was busy in the garden.

Sasha said, 'She is nice, but she's several years older than he is and I'm sure his offer was made out of kindness, no other motive.'

Her tone of voice was, to Rosie, a clear signal that Tom should get off this subject.

His masculine ear being less finely attuned to such nuances, he went on, 'With a big place like El Monasterio to keep up, he needs someone really capable...keen on cooking and gardening. A girl like either of you would be useless.'

'Charming! Thanks very much,' Sasha said tartly.

'I only meant useless domestically. It's not that you two couldn't cook and garden if you put your minds to it. But neither of you wants to, or only as a sideline, the way men do those things. You'd both rather do your *own* thing. I used to disapprove of that. Now I've come to terms with it.'

'Nick may never have shared your prejudices. I think we should leave him to sort out his life for himself and concentrate on the plans for our wedding,' Sasha said firmly.

Presently, leaving them to make all the decisions a wedding involved, Rosie left for the office.

Throughout the morning she worked in her usual quick, methodical way. After lunch, last night's excess of champagne and waking up in the small hours and not getting back to sleep until about five began to take their toll.

Although it was rare for her to leave early, at half-past three she knocked off and took a taxi to South Molton Street. There, or in St Christopher's Place on the other side of Oxford Street, she would be sure to find something to wear at the wedding.

She had long ago learned what suited her and what didn't, and by half-past four she had acquired two large carriers and was feeling like a cup of tea. She went to the Justin de Blank café which was not far away and where they had chocolate brownies as good as her mother's. It was one of those days when her taste-buds craved something sinful.

As she drank her tea, she admitted to herself that it was because Nick was coming to the wedding that she had just spent a lot of money on a new outfit when there were several which would have done in her wardrobe.

The discovery that the divine Madame Clermont was far too old to play the part in his life she had thought she did was an enormous relief. But now, stupidly, she had made Nick believe there was a man in the background of her own life. How was she to disabuse him of that idea without proving herself a liar?

The night before Sasha's wedding, Rosie gave a party for her.

Nick and Madame Clermont had arrived in London that morning and were staying at the Pelham Hotel in Cromwell Place. They were spending a week in London before going to Paris together. According to Sasha, he thought Marie-Laure too frail to revisit that city on her own.

While they were away, Tom and Sasha were going to return to Font Vella for their honeymoon. After which they would leave for Australia and a new life together.

So the party was the last many of Sasha's friends would see of her except if she came back to Europe for a holiday, but that was unlikely to be for a long time.

As usual, Clare had taken responsibility for all the preparations for the party. Rosie had come home from

work to find everything under control and nothing
for her to do but have a bath and dress.

From the moment when Nick's flight was due to
land, she had felt a mounting excitement because he
was in the same country, not at a safe distance in
Spain.

As she reached behind her to fasten her pale grey
silk taffeta dress which, with its lace collar and cuffs,
looked demure, even prim from the front but was cut
to show off her back, she glanced at the clock by her
bed.

In less than half an hour the guests would start ar-
riving and Nick and the Frenchwoman might be
among the first comers. How, *how* was she to undo
that fatal mistake she had made the last time they
spoke on the telephone?

In fact there were about a dozen people in the
flower-bedecked living-room when some sixth sense
told her that the only guest who mattered a whit to
her had arrived.

Standing at the far end of the room, she turned her
head and saw Tom and Sasha, who had stationed
themselves near the door to welcome everyone,
greeting a woman of outstanding elegance.

Although it was a warm summer evening, coming
from a hotter climate and being built with the graceful
slenderness of a whippet, Marie-Laure Clermont had
chosen to dress in a dark red velvet like the petals of
Clare's favourite roses.

Rosie could tell at a glance that the dress must be
half a century old, not only because it was cut in the
style of the Thirties but because such velvet, supple
silk velvet, was no longer made even for the great
couture houses.

The rich colour set off to perfection its wearer's sugar-white hair. Her thin hands, weighted with perhaps a dozen rings, were brown. But her face she must keep protected from the sun's rays, for it was much paler, and her make-up was put on with great discretion so that she did not have the mask-like visage of some of her generation.

Behind her, Nick, in black tie, looked so compellingly attractive that Rosie felt herself tremble inwardly.

She said, 'Would you excuse me?' to the group she had been talking to and went to be presented to Madame Clermont.

'This is my great friend Rosie Middleton, Marie-Laure,' said Sasha.

'How do you do, *madame*? Having seen your house in Font Vella and read about you in Nick's book, it's a great pleasure to welcome you to this house,' said Rosie, holding out her hand.

The claw-like fingers which gripped it were unexpectedly warm and strong.

'And for me to be here, Miss Middleton. But as we are both close friends of this one——' her other hand fastened on Nick's arm '—shall we be informal and call each other by our first names?'

Rosie smiled and nodded, then raised her eyes to meet his. 'Hello, Nick.'

'Good evening. You're looking very beautiful tonight.'

'Thank you.'

His compliment gave her no pleasure. She recognised it for what it was, a smooth piece of flattery, suitable to the occasion but not sincere or only to the extent that he liked her dress.

He did not like her any more. She felt sure of it. Perhaps he was piqued that she preferred to cycle in France with another man than to visit him in Spain, making up—although he had not explained that—a foursome with Sasha and Tom.

A student Clare had hired to help with the drinks was hovering with a tray of champagne. Bright enough to realise that the lady in red was a *grande dame*, he bowed slightly as he offered it to her.

'Thank you.' Her rings flashing as she took a glass, Marie-Laure gave him a smile which acknowledged that he was a nice-looking young man with whom, if sixty years younger, she would enjoy a flirtation. And he, perhaps having had his fill of girls of his own age playing it cool and offhand, reacted with a blushing grin.

'Did you have a good flight? Is your hotel comfortable?' asked Rosie as they moved further into the room to make way for more arrivals.

'A marvellous flight and the hotel is delightful, like a private house of excellent style and comfort. I have a suite on the first floor which might be in a *château*. But don't let me keep you from your duties as hostess. I am not one of those old ladies who leaves a party early to say her prayers and go to bed. I am a night owl. There will be time to talk later.'

'I certainly hope so,' said Rosie. 'But let me introduce—— '

'Not at all necessary,' Marie-Laure interrupted. 'First I shall look round your drawing-room at all your things, which are of great interest to me, and then I shall cast my eye over your guests and introduce myself to those I think might be interesting. Off you go, pretty Rosie.'

Amused by her guest's forthrightness, and pleased with this second compliment which she did not doubt *was* sincere because the Frenchwoman had the air of a person who, although she might never be unkind, would never utter false praise, Rosie did as she was told.

It was not until supper was served at nine o'clock that she felt that the guests had had enough hostessly attention and that from now on she could relax and, while still keeping a watchful eye out for glasses which needed replenishing, enjoy herself.

There were plenty of places for everyone to sit comfortably, although some had to balance their plates on their laps, using the large Victorian double damask napkins Clare had bought at a jumble sale, to protect their clothes.

As she finished making her selection from the array of dishes Clare had prepared for the buffet and looked round for a place to sit—most people were already eating—Rosie saw that all the seats in the living-room were occupied.

She went downstairs to the overflow areas and saw, in the TV room, her housekeeper next to Nick. Quickly she turned away, finding a place for herself between two guests at the eating end of the kitchen.

It was unlike Clare to sit down before everyone else had been served. Perhaps she had only done so because Nick had insisted. Could it be that Tom was right and he was interested in her?

He was certainly among the most active helpers when the time came to clear away the main course and encourage people to help themselves to the puddings. Rosie noticed him helping her again at the coffee stage, taking cups round on a tray and later removing them. Did he always make himself useful at parties where it was necessary? Or was he exerting himself as a special service to Clare?

Oh, God, what does it matter why he's doing it? she asked herself impatiently. One thing is certain: it isn't for *my* sake. He hasn't spared me a glance since he arrived. I might not exist for all the notice he's taken of me since we said hello.

After she had rung for a cab for a couple who had to leave early and gone to the door with them when it arrived, she saw Marie-Laure beckoning to her from a sofa.

'Tomorrow night, the honeymooners will be on their way to Spain and you will be on your own. I should like you to come and dine with me at the hotel. Will you?'

'It's very kind of you, but——'

'You are thinking of your other friend . . . the one who keeps house for you . . . that she may feel lonely.'

'Yes.'

'I am told she will be going to a concert with her daughter.'

Clare hadn't mentioned this, but nor had Rosie asked what she planned to do after the wedding. She had assumed they would put their feet up together.

'In that case I'd like to dine with you. Will Nick be there?'

'Where else?' The old lady chuckled. 'He may be annoyed with me.'

'Annoyed? Why?'

'For usurping his privilege. Surely it is the custom, in this as in other countries, for the bride's chief attendant, if unmarried, to dine with the best man?'

'I believe it's usual, yes, although as this wedding is going to be very informal I am not really a bridesmaid in the ordinary sense.'

'You are Sasha's closest and best friend. She spoke of you with great affection while she was staying in Spain.'

'We've known each other a long time.'

'And Nick and Tom also, I understand?'

'We knew them a long time ago. We haven't kept in touch although, as you probably know, Tom and Sasha were in love in those days.'

'And then quarrelled and were apart until Nick brought them together. Yes, I have heard their story. But you, Rosie...you felt no *tendresse* for my dear Nicholas when you knew him before?'

There was great kindness and wisdom in Marie-Laure's shrewd dark eyes and Rosie longed to confide in her. At the same time she was afraid that if she admitted to tender feelings for Nick, not only in the past but now, the Frenchwoman might pass on the information. That was a humiliation she could not risk.

'I have always wanted, more than anything, to be my own mistress,' she answered. 'Perhaps, one day, someone's wife but, before that, a woman of independent means. It may seem a strange ambition to someone of your generation but it's the way I am.'

'*Ma chère*, you surely do not imagine that the wish to be independent is something new? Women have always wanted to stand on their own feet, but sometimes it has been impossible. I am of the opinion that it is better to remain single than to be married to a man who is dull or difficult. But there are some men in the world—a rather rare species, I fear—who have much to offer a woman. When one of those comes along then one should exert oneself to capture his interest. For me there were three such men and each one became my husband. Nicholas is such a man. But alas I am far too old to captivate him.'

Rosie said lightly, 'Have you no granddaughters who would suit him?'

'Unfortunately I never had children, but in any case I suspect—I am not sure, but I suspect—that he has someone in mind but there are certain...obstacles. How tall he is, and how well he carries himself.'

She was gazing down the length of the room and, looking in the same direction, Rosie saw Nick in conversation with a freelance photographer who was a friend of Sasha's. Clare was with them, attending closely to whatever Nick was saying.

The light from a nearby table-lamp was casting an upward glow on his face, now even more deeply tanned than earlier in the year, the mahogany shade of his skin emphasised by the whiteness of his dress shirt in the same way that his wing collar underlined the cleanly cut lines of his jaw and chin.

Almost as if he sensed that he was being watched from afar, he turned and looked towards them, his vivid eyes meeting Rosie's briefly before shifting to her companion. It was at Marie-Laure that he smiled.

A few moments later he came to join them. 'It's been a long day, *ma chère*. I know you like to keep late hours but perhaps, with a wedding tomorrow, we should go back to the hotel now. By the time we have talked and drunk a little cognac together it will be past midnight.'

'I think you are right. We should leave. Tomorrow night there is another pleasure in store. Our pretty hostess is coming to dine with us.'

Nick did not look as if the prospect pleased him particularly.

He said in a matter-of-fact tone, 'Good: it will be an opportunity to discuss my proposal to buy Sasha's share of the house. She has mentioned it to you, I believe?'

'Yes,' said Rosie. 'She has, and it seems a very good idea.'

'I'm glad you think so. We'll go into the details tomorrow. Now, if you could ring for a taxi...'

CHAPTER TEN

THAT night Rosie dreamt of another party, long ago.

Stored in her subconscious mind was a detailed memory of the Christmas Eve after-work party in a pub near the *News* office, at the end of which Nick had taken her round rosy face between his hands and dropped a casual kiss on her closed lips under the mistletoe.

But in her dream it was different. In real life she had stood there, flabbergasted with delight and confusion, while he patted her cheeks and said 'Happy Christmas, Rosie. Don't OD on Christmas pud.'

By then, although new to the job, she had learned from the routine calls to the police and fire stations, made every day by one of the junior reporters, that OD meant overdose.

But she hadn't minded his teasing because—or so she had thought—it was the loving teasing she got from her family, not the unkind teasing she had sometimes received at school.

It had been her first kiss, the light push needed to propel her across the boundary of hero-worship into the raptures of first love.

But in her dream she was not a theoretically knowledgeable but actually extremely innocent seventeen-year-old. She was herself as she was now, and when Nick bent to kiss her she slipped her arms round his neck in eager response.

For a few heavenly seconds their lips met in a passionate kiss until suddenly Nick grabbed her wrists and jerked down her arms.

'For God's sake, Rosie, what kind of behaviour is this? You know how I feel about Clare. Haven't you any loyalty to her after all she's done for you?'

With which he stalked out of the pub, leaving her scarlet with embarrassment as everyone else deliberately turned their backs on her.

She woke up, knowing at once that it was only a dream, yet with her heart still beating from the feel of his strong arms around her, the exciting roughness of his six o'clock chin rasping her softer skin, and the fleeting ardour of his kiss.

To dispel the illusion she reached out to turn on her light. Tonight she had brought up to bed a half-full bottle of spring water. There was some left. She sat up, filled the tumbler and reached over the side of the bed to retrieve the two reading pillows she had thrown out before going to sleep.

For a while she sat sipping the water and thinking about the man now asleep at the Pelham and the woman sleeping upstairs and wondering if Clare was the reason Nick's manner towards herself had become noticeably cool.

Between the ages of ten and eighteen, Rosie had been a bridesmaid at all the village church weddings of her brothers, sisters and cousins.

Privately she found Sasha's and Tom's short civil ceremony in a register office rather soulless.

Afterwards Sasha's parents gave a small informal lunch party at the hotel where they were staying. Their guests were the bridegroom's father, a widower, the

best man, Rosie, Clare and her daughter Angie, and
Madame Clermont. At two-thirty the newlyweds left
for the airport and the party broke up.

'I'm going to have a nap. Otherwise I might fall
asleep at the concert tonight, and that would never
do,' said Clare, as they entered the house where all
traces of last night's party had been tidied up early
that morning.

'I might lie down too,' said Rosie. 'I found chatting
to the parents rather an effort. How odd that they
should have produced Sasha and Tom. I found them
terribly dull.'

Her remark reminded her of telling Carolyn, Nick's
editor, that journalists were never bored by anyone.
Perhaps Mr and Mrs Otley and Tom's father were the
exceptions to the rule, or perhaps she was off form
today.

'They were rather stiff and inarticulate, weren't
they?' Clare agreed, beginning to mount the stairs.
'I'll set my alarm clock for five and bring you some
tea. That will give us plenty of time to get ready for
the evening.'

But in the event it was Rosie, who, unable to sleep,
had spent the afternoon reading, who took a tea-tray
up to Clare's eyrie at the top of the house.

Evidently Clare had slept until the alarm clock woke
her a few minutes earlier. She was still lying in bed,
a little flushed, her hair not as neat as usual. It made
her look younger.

'How kind of you, Rosie,' she said, hoisting herself
into a sitting position.

'We haven't had much chance to talk about Nick's
proposal to lend you the money to buy Sasha's share

of the house,' said Rosie. 'Is this a suitable moment or are you still half asleep?'

'No, no. I went out like a light, but I'm wide awake now. Pull up that chair.' Clare indicated a small tub chair she had bought for a song and re-covered with a remnant of chintz.

While Rosie was pouring out tea, she went on, 'It's an extraordinarily generous offer on Nick's part. I can't think why he should be so kind. He's also suggested that, while he's away in July, Angie and I should have a holiday at his house in Spain.'

'Where is he going in July?'

'To stay with friends in Italy. He seems to have friends all over the world. Not surprising really. He's such a dear. I can't imagine anyone not liking him. Not many men of his age would trouble to escort an old lady to Paris. He didn't say so himself, but from what Madame Clermont told me most of her contemporaries have died off and going back might be quite painful for her if he were not going to be there to dispel the sadness for her.'

'So you're in favour of his plan?' said Rosie, in agreement with Clare's encomium but finding it hard to listen to her singing Nick's praises.

'Yes, indeed I am. But are you? What he proposes is that I should move downstairs into Sasha's bedroom and Angie into what is now the darkroom, and this part of the house should become a self-contained flat for visitors, including himself. But perhaps you would rather we stayed where we are and Sasha's room became the visitors' room with the darkroom changed to a bathroom?'

'I think his plan is best. I know anything goes nowadays but I have a conventional streak and I shouldn't feel comfortable with the alternative,' said Rosie. 'And anyway I should like to have you and Angie sharing with me, if you won't mind having less privacy? I shall miss Sasha less with you downstairs. So that's settled, all but the legal and financial details. I gather Nick wanted you to dine with us tonight if you hadn't had tickets for a concert. What concert is it?'

'It's Robert Southwold conducting Holst's *Planets* at the Barbican Hall. He's been giving special tutorials to selected students at the college and Angie thinks he's wonderful.'

'From what I hear he is a marvellous conductor. I'm an ignoramus about serious music but even I have heard of Southwold. Is he living in England now? I thought Switzerland was his base.'

'It was, but it seems his father is gravely ill and won't live much longer. Robert Southwold has been in England, comforting his mother, since the condition was diagnosed. His parents were in their forties when he was born so they're both very old and frail. I shouldn't think his mother will last long after his father goes.'

'What about his own family. Are they over here too?'

'He isn't married,' Clare told her. 'I should think it's virtually impossible to combine the schedule of an internationally famous conductor with a normal domestic life. He is dedicated to music. I've never heard his name linked with any women.'

'Perhaps he prefers his own sex.'

'There's nothing like that about him.' Clare sounded quite indignant.

'It wasn't meant as a slur,' Rosie said pacifyingly.
'More tea?'

'Yes, please. What are you wearing tonight?'

'My taupe silk. And you?'

Their conversation turned to the clothes worn at
last night's party and at the wedding and remained
on that subject until it was time to bath and change
for the evening.

Clare and her daughter, who had left the wedding
party early to attend a class, set out for their concert
an hour before it was necessary for Rosie to leave.

She was ready to go and was having a glass of wine
and thinking about the newlyweds, who by now might
be watching the sun set from the *mirador*, when the
doorbell rang.

She opened the door to find Carl in the porch.

It was unheard of for him to turn up uninvited but
she saw at once that he wasn't his usual self. In her
newspaper days she had seen too many people re-
acting to various kinds of trouble, from bereavements
to house fires, not to recognise the signs that something bad had happened to him, and very recently.

'Carl! Come in...is something the matter?' she
asked, stepping back to admit him.

'You can say that again! I've been fired. Me and
five others. Since the take-over last month there's been
what's called "a rationalisation". In plain language,
six jobs have been axed. Rationalisation, my foot. The
word I'd use is bloodbath. I need a stiff drink,
Rosie...and a shoulder to cry on.'

By now it was apparent that several stiff drinks were
already circulating in his bloodstream.

'How about a nice cup of tea and something to eat?' she suggested, stepping back to let him come in.

She could see she was going to have to ring the Pelham Hotel and ask them to give Madame Clermont her apologies and say she had been delayed but would get there as soon as possible.

She had known other people who had been the helpless victims of mergers and take-overs. She knew what a bombshell it was suddenly to be out in the cold, often with heavy financial commitments which had to be met or total disaster would ensue. As he had no wife and children, Carl's position was not as desperate as that, but the blow to his pride and confidence must be tremendous.

He was a friend she had neglected of late, but that didn't mean she could turn him away when he was in urgent need of someone to sympathise with him.

'What delayed you?' Nick asked rather curtly, when she was shown into the sitting-room of Madame Clermont's suite, full of apologies for keeping them waiting.

'A friend turned up unexpectedly and then I had difficulty getting a taxi.'

'Nick wanted to come and fetch you but I restrained him,' said Marie-Laure. 'It is really of no importance what time we dine,' she added soothingly. 'Sit down and relax, my dear. It is always excessively awkward when people arrive at inopportune moments. Nick will get you a drink.'

Thank God she had restrained him, thought Rosie. If he had come to the house he would have found Carl dead to the world on the sofa where he had collapsed while Rosie was down in the kitchen making tea and Welsh rarebit, the best quick hot snack she could think of for a man who had had a liquid lunch.

At first he had sat in the kitchen with her and begun to talk about his troubles. Then he had excused himself to sway to the loo and from there, being far from clear-headed, had gone back up to the living-room, there to pour himself the hefty slug which had knocked him out.

In a way she had been relieved to find him collapsed on a sofa. He would probably still be asleep when she returned. Meanwhile she had loosened his tie, removed his shoes and covered him with a blanket.

She had left a note beside him, in case he woke, and another note for Clare and Angie who had never met Carl and would naturally be puzzled if they returned to find an unknown man sleeping off a binge in the living-room. But with any luck she would be back long before they were.

Possibly sensing that her guest was a good deal less calm than she was trying to appear, Marie-Laure embarked on a series of amusing anecdotes which, judging by the spontaneity of his laughter, were new to Nick as well as to Rosie.

Soon the evening was going with a swing and Nick seemed more like his old self, by which Rosie meant the way he had been during her weekend at Font Vella with Anna and Carolyn.

'Why don't you two young people finish this happy day as we did at the end of the Twenties when I was young?' suggested Marie-Laure.

Dinner was over. A dish of handmade chocolates had been brought for them to nibble with the coffee, served in elegant porcelain demitasses, but now the chocolates were eaten, the coffee-pot empty.

'How was that?' Nick asked her, smiling.

'We would go to a nightclub to dance. Oh, how we danced! The tango, the Charleston, the foxtrot... wonderful dances, wonderful music. Surely there must be somewhere in London for a close friend of the bridegroom to take a close friend of the bride?'

'I'm sure there is. Would you like that, Rosie?' he asked.

Was he merely being polite? Fulfilling his final duty as the best man? Yet his eyes seemed to hold the same warm glint she remembered from the afternoon when he had scooped her into his arms in a secluded corner of the garden at the monastery.

For a moment she was tempted to say there was nothing she would like more, and then she remembered Carl and forced herself to answer, 'Any other night I should have liked to go dancing, but not tonight.'

'Why not tonight?'

'I—I have an important meeting early tomorrow and these last few days have been so busy that I haven't prepared for it as well as I should have done.'

'Well I'd hate to interfere with the onward and upward progress of your career,' Nick said, with a hint of sarcasm. 'I'd better take you home.'

'It's kind of you, but quite unnecessary.'

'Nick is right. At this time of night, in London, I think he should go with you,' said Marie-Laure. 'One reads of deplorable things happening to unprotected women. How different it was in the Twenties. Then one could stroll where one pleased in full evening dress and jewels. It was a wonderful time to be young.'

'If you were rich,' Nick said drily.

'I was rich then,' she agreed. 'Or my father was. But now I am poor. I shouldn't be staying here if you had not insisted on paying the bill, *mon cher*.' She turned a mischievous smile on Rosie. 'One of the compensations of my great age is that I can no longer be compromised, as we called it in my day. I doubt if you even know what that expression means.'

'Oh, but I do,' said Rosie. 'When I was twelve and thirteen I used to spend hours reading novels belonging to Granny, some of them years old. The heroines were always getting themselves compromised. I think those days must have been rather restful and nice.'

'You'd have hated them,' Nick told her flatly. 'Your only options would have been marriage or spinsterhood, which would have meant staying at home, helping your mother.'

'I don't agree. I should have stood on my own feet no matter what period I had lived in,' she retorted with spirit, annoyed by his crack about her career.

'But you will let Nick see you home . . . if only to please me,' the old lady pressed her gently.

The figurative clash of swords which had just taken place seemed to amuse her. Her dark eyes were twinkling.

'If Nick puts me into a taxi I shall be perfectly safe. Clare may be back before me. Thank you for a nice evening. I hope you enjoy the rest of your time here . . . and in Paris.'

Although they had met for the first time little more than twenty-four hours ago, Rosie bent to kiss her goodnight.

A taxi had just brought a middle-aged couple and their luggage to the hotel's porticoed entrance. Nick and Rosie stood by while the cases were taken by a porter, the fare paid and goodnights exchanged.

Then Nick gave the driver her address and Rosie stepped into the back and sat down next to the door, leaning forward to bid him goodnight before he closed the door for her.

Instead she was forced to jerk back as Nick dipped his tall head and followed her in, pulling the door shut behind him.

'There's really no need——' she began.

'I think there is...if only to put Marie-Laure's mind at rest.'

At this point the driver, behind whom the glass panel had been open, reached backwards to slide it shut, sealing them into the curiously private world of the back of a London taxi after dark.

'Don't worry,' Nick said. 'I shall behave impeccably...as if we were back in the Twenties when the only things that happened in taxis were proposals of marriage and a little light necking.'

He slid his tall form into the opposite corner where he sat slightly sideways to give maximum room to his long legs. This time there was no mistaking the bite of sarcasm in his voice.

'I never imagined otherwise,' Rosie said coolly.

'No? In that case why were you so anxious for me not to come with you?'

'Simply to save you the trouble.'

'Since when has it been a trouble for a man to see an attractive girl home? We're not taking the last bus to darkest Wimbledon and I shan't have to walk back,' he said drily, adding, 'Although I probably shall, for the exercise.'

'I don't think that would be wise...not in a dinner-jacket. This isn't rural Spain.'

'Nor is it the lower east side of Manhattan.'

Seizing the chance to sidestep personal topics, she said, 'Have you spent much time in New York?'

'I've been there a couple of times. Have you?'

'Only once. I thought it was a marvellous city.'

'You would. It's a mecca for career girls and seethes with ambitious women competing for the top jobs.'

'I don't know why you have the impression that my job is the only thing which matters to me.'

'Isn't it?'

No, you are...damn you! she thought.

Aloud, she said, 'No more than your career as a writer is to you. And I'm in a position you have never been in...I employ several people. If I fall down on my job, they will be out of work, which is no joke.'

Reminded of Carl, who was now in that unhappy state, she wondered if he were still sleeping or had woken with a splitting head and was at this moment rummaging around for aspirins.

What on earth was she going to do if Nick insisted on coming in with her? A thought occurred which was like biting on a tooth with an exposed nerve. It was possible that he was here with her now because he hoped to see Clare.

He said, 'OK, let's come to terms. I won't make any more cracks about your career if you'll get it out of your head that I'm an inveterate womaniser. I'm not.'

'All right...agreed.'

'Shake on it?' He extended his right hand.

She put her hand into his. As his fingers closed over hers, a slow shiver of pleasure ran through her. If he could do this to her merely by holding her hand, what would she feel if he took her in his arms and kissed her?

She knew then that what she longed for, more than anything in the world, was to arrive at her house, invite Nick in for a drink and keep him there for a night of unimaginable bliss.

But that was impossible on two counts. Carl might still be there and, even if he had woken up and gone home, it wouldn't be long before Clare and Angie returned. The only person who, if there had been no other obstacles, would not have interfered with that lovely but impossible consummation of a ten-year-old dream was Marie-Laure.

She was much too worldly wise to worry if Nick failed to return to the hotel. Rosie felt sure that she knew, without being told, how Rosie felt about Nick and, had she been in her place, would have used all her arts to enchant him. She had said as much last night at the party.

But apart from the fact that Rosie knew she lacked the qualities which made women irresistible, she also felt times had changed since Marie-Laure had been her age. Then, women competed for men far more ruthlessly because their futures hinged on whom they married. Whether their lives were easy and interesting or hard and dreary had depended on their husbands. That was no longer so. And it was no longer 'on' to lure a man into bed when he seemed to be drawn to another woman who might make him a much better wife.

Anyway there could be no question of tacitly inviting Nick to stay with her tonight, Rosie thought glumly as the taxi approached her road. If the light was still on in the living-room she would know that Carl was still prostrate on the sofa.

To her dismay, when they arrived at her house, not only was light showing through the living-room curtains but the first-floor rooms, were alight although not those on the floor above.

'Do you always leave all your lights on?' Nick asked, as he stepped out and glanced at the house before turning to help her alight.

'I came away in a hurry. Thank you for bringing me back. Goodnight, Nick.'

'I'll see you inside.' He bent to the nearside window and handed the driver some notes.

'There aren't any muggers around. You're fussing,' Rosie protested. 'Please keep the taxi. Marie-Laure will be waiting for you.'

'No, she won't. I'm coming in. I want to talk to you.'

'What about? Can't it wait till tomorrow? I've got work to do.'

'So you said, but I don't believe you.' He handed the driver a tip, put the other coins in his pocket, said, 'Thanks...goodnight,' and took a firm hold of Rosie's arm above the elbow.

Torn between wanting to know what it was he wanted to talk about and nervous about what the lights upstairs portended, she saw it was useless to argue. He was determined to come in.

CHAPTER ELEVEN

'Women living in cities are advised to have their latch-keys ready before they arrive at their doors,' Nick said, as Rosie fumbled in her bag while slowly mounting the steps up to the front door.

'On my own I do have it ready.'

Her evening bag was smaller and less well organised than her day bag. Damn! Why did the wretched key have to elude her tonight of all nights?

When she found it, Nick took it from her and unlocked the door which, Carl being there, she had not double-locked as they usually did when leaving the house empty.

He pushed the door open and waited for her to precede him. Two steps inside she could see that Carl was no longer lying on the sofa, nor was her note propped against the lamp base on the table near his head.

She had removed the empty whisky glass before she went out, but there was a distinct whiff of whisky in the air. She hoped Nick would think it was left over from last night's party.

Where was Carl? Had he woken, gone to the upstairs loo, forgetting there was one in the basement, and then flaked out on her bed or Sasha's? Sober, he was not a man who did things like that. But badly hung-over, perhaps he might. At any rate he wasn't snoring. Perhaps, if she kept cool, this contretemps would blow over.

'You look like a schoolgirl who's been summoned to the headmistress's study, Rosie. What are you expecting? A lecture? That's not what I have in mind,' Nick said, smiling slightly.

What *did* he have in mind? That lift at the corner of his mouth made her even more uneasy.

She said, 'Let's have another drink. I'll have a brandy and ginger. I think the ice tub is empty. You know where the fridge is, don't you? Would you mind filling it while I go upstairs to turn off the lights I left on.'

Nick moved to the drinks tray, picked up the insulated tub and was turning towards the stairs going down to the basement when there was a sound from above.

She recognised it at once as the noise made by the pedal-bin in the bathroom when the lid was released and fell back on to the bin. To him it was a sound which he did not expect to hear in an empty house.

'Are you sure *you* left the lights on?' he asked, in an undertone.

'Certain... it's a failing of mine.' She crossed to the foot of the stairs, ignoring Nick's, 'Stay where you are. I'll take a look.'

Their drinks table was at the other end of the living-room and, as he strode towards her, Carl emerged from the landing door of the bathroom. Seeing Rosie looking up at him, he said, 'I've been taking a bath in your spa tub. You two girls believe in pampering yourselves.'

He began to come down the stairs just as Nick reached the newel post. Carl stopped short, looking surprised. Obviously it hadn't occurred to him that someone might have brought her home.

Nick's face had become a hard mask of angular bone and taut flesh, all expression erased except from his eyes which turned from Carl to her with a look which made her heart sink.

There was a pause which seemed endless. Then Rosie pulled herself together. 'This is Carl, the friend I told you about, who arrived unexpectedly just as I was leaving. I told him to make himself at home until I or the others came back. Carl, this is——'

'Nick Winchester,' Carl supplied, coming down and holding out his hand.

A sleep followed by a bath had sobered him up. He looked back to normal, a bit heavy-eyed perhaps, but spruce and in full control of himself, not the verging on legless, distraught man who had come to her for sympathy a few hours earlier.

'I've often seen you on TV,' he said, offering Nick his hand. 'I didn't know Rosie knew you.'

Nick shook hands with him. 'Rosie plays her cards very close to her chest. Who knows who she knows? Are you the guy she's going cycling in France with?' He looked down at her. 'Or is that someone else?'

'It's not me,' said Carl. 'I haven't been on a bike since I left school. A colleague of mine...a former colleague, I should say——' he interpolated in a wry tone '—went with a group of bikers down the west coast of France last summer. There was an interpreter in charge and a van to carry their luggage between the overnight stops. Is that what you're doing, Rosie?'

'No, her trip is for two people only,' Nick informed him. 'It's time I was getting back. I'm sure Carl will be happy to fix your drink for you, Rosie. Good-night, Carl. I won't say it was nice meeting you, but it was enlightening.'

With a brief, arctic glance at her and another clipped, 'Goodnight,' he let himself out.

In silence they listened to his footsteps going down the path which no longer led to a gate because, like that of many London houses, what had been a small front garden was now a paved parking area for two cars.

As the sound of Nick's long-legged stride died away down the street, Carl said, 'Hell, now I've bust up your love-life. I'm sorry about that, Rosie. If I'd known he was here I'd have kept quiet and stayed upstairs. Still, that might have made matters worse...if he'd come upstairs and found me lurking in your bedroom.'

'He wouldn't have come upstairs. You haven't bust up my love-life. All that's happened is that an acquaintance has jumped to a false conclusion. It couldn't matter less,' said Rosie. 'I'll fix you something to eat, Carl.'

'I've had an Alka Seltzer I found in your bathroom cupboard. That's all my stomach can take at the moment, thanks. I don't know how to apologise for reeling in here like some broken-down wino. I'm sorry...I'm really sorry.'

'So you keep saying, quite unnecessarily. At least have a cup of coffee while we talk about what you should do next.'

'My head's still too thick for clear thinking, but a cup of coffee would be good. Then I'll leave you in peace.'

They were down in the kitchen, drinking coffee and, partly to take her mind off her own problems, Rosie was encouraging him to talk when they heard Clare and Angie come in.

Rather surprisingly, they did not come down to the kitchen but went straight up to their flat.

About half an hour later, Rosie fetched Carl's coat and tie which he had left in her bedroom where he had undressed before his bath. Then he set out to walk to his flat, saying the exercise would do him good.

Feeling suddenly very weary, she double-locked the front door and plodded upstairs to bed. But, as she had known it would be, she found it impossible to sleep.

What had Nick wanted to talk to her about? Had his goodnight meant goodbye? Would he ask Bury & Poole to cancel their agreement with her and get another agency to handle the promotion of his book?

The most likely answer to the last two questions was yes. The answer to the first was something she might never find out.

The only faint gleam of cheer in the situation was that it did seem to scotch her idea that he was interested in Clare. If that were the case, why should he care how many men there were in Rosie's life?

Very early the following morning, Rosie received a call from the mother of her senior assistant. Her daughter had been taken ill during the night and was not fit to come to work. She appeared to be suffering from food poisoning, perhaps caused by a meal in a restaurant the previous evening. The doctor would be called to see her as soon as the surgery opened.

'I can handle everything she was going to do today. I'll call you tonight to see how she is. Give her my best and tell her not to worry about a thing except getting better,' said Rosie.

Her assistant's commitments included taking an author to Bristol for a couple of women's page interviews and a 'down the line' radio interview, which meant that the author would be in a studio in Bristol answering questions from an interviewer in another studio in Bath.

It was late in the evening when she got home.

'Sasha called. They've been basking by the pool all day. She sounded blissfully happy and sent you her love,' said Clare, coming downstairs, having heard the taxi draw up.

Tired as she was, Rosie noticed at once that there was something different about her housekeeper. Perhaps she had changed her make-up or it was the new blouse she was wearing which was particularly becoming. Rosie had never seen her looking better.

'Any other messages?' she asked.

'Nick came round about five. I said you had planned to work late and gave him the office number. Did he call you?'

Rosie shook her head. 'What did he want?'

'He didn't say.'

'Did he stay long?'

'About an hour. I offered him a drink in case you should change your mind and come home from the station instead of going to the office. Then Angie came in and he had quite a long chat with her. She's taken a tremendous shine to him, you know, although he doesn't rate quite as highly in her pantheon of heroes as Robert Southwold.'

'How was the concert?'

'Superb,' Clare enthused. 'We had supper afterwards with one of Angie's friends and her parents. It was a really nice evening.'

'I heard you come in and expected to hear all about it last night,' said Rosie.

'You don't always want us butting in,' said Clare. 'Your supper's all ready. Shrimp bisque and cottage cheese salad. It won't take long to heat the soup.'

Rosie's assistant was off sick all that week, which kept her extremely busy. Nick made no further attempt to get in touch with her. She suspected that he hadn't intended to contact her but had made that an excuse to see her housekeeper. During the week he saw Clare again to finalise the arrangements to do with his lending her the money to pay Sasha.

Guessing that Marie-Laure would regard it as a lapse of good manners if she did not receive a formal letter from her, Rosie had found time in Bristol to choose an attractive card—a reproduction of a painting by Tissot of a young cavalry officer with a waxed moustache and a red stripe down the leg of his tight dress trousers—and to compose a graceful expression of thanks.

The following Monday, she received a note written, in an ornate but clear hand, on the hotel's writing paper and dated the previous Saturday.

Ma chère,

I was delighted with your choice of card. I'm so glad you enjoyed your evening with us. Very few young people take the trouble to write but it is much appreciated by people of my generation. We leave London tomorrow. I hope I

shall not regret revisiting Paris for the first time
in many years. I hope to see you again before
too long although Nicholas tells me that when
we return to Spain he must seclude himself until
the new book is finished. It seems likely to
occupy him until the autumn. He sends his
regards.

Had he really sent his regards or was that a mere
politesse added by Marie-Laure? Rosie wondered.

During the short time between her return from her
honeymoon and her departure for Australia, Sasha
and Clare signed the papers which made Clare the
new co-owner of the house.

On their last night in England, Tom took Clare and
Angie to the cinema, leaving his wife and her friend
to spend the evening alone together.

'It's funny the way things have turned out. Tom
always seemed such a stick-in-the-mud, the last person
to go gallivanting off to Australia,' said Sasha, while
they were having supper *à deux* at the table in the
kitchen.

'Australia is getting nearer every year. By the end
of the century, they say, it'll only take a few hours to
fly from London to Sydney.'

'But you'll come and see us soon, won't you?'

'Of course,' said Rosie. 'Probably next
winter...maybe for Christmas.'

Thinking of next winter reminded her of Bury &
Poole's sales conference in Spain in the autumn. To
her personal and professional relief, Nick had not
asked for her to be replaced. Only that morning Anna

had telephoned to ask her to handle another important book coming out some months after his.

Evidently he was in Sasha's thoughts too. She said, 'I'm glad that, thanks to Nick, you're not having to share the house with a stranger...not yet anyway.'

'What do you mean...not yet?'

'I've noticed a definite glow about Clare since we came back. Usually, when a woman suddenly starts buying clothes and trying out new hairstyles, it's because of a man.'

'Clare isn't going out on dates. She's out tonight and she went to a concert with Angie recently, but otherwise she's always in in the evenings. She goes out by herself during the day but I doubt if she meets a man.'

'I think she may have fallen for Nick,' said Sasha. 'Would you mind that, Rosie?'

Mind? It would break my heart, she thought.

But not even to Sasha could Rosie confide the misery she had been suffering since Nick had walked out of the house.

She forced herself to say, 'I think Clare is probably the ideal person to run his monastery for him. She would love the garden. Ours is too small to give her much scope.'

'I'm not so sure Nick is interested in her,' said Sasha. 'With men it's harder to tell.'

'The fact that he's just lent her a very large sum of money tells you something, doesn't it?'

'He could have done that for your sake?'

'Mine? How do you work that out?'

'To save you having to find a replacement for me. Finding a house partner is almost as tricky as finding a life partner.'

'I think his motive was to secure a problem-free *pied-à-terre* for himself,' said Rosie, refilling their wine glasses. 'Anyway, if something develops between those two, I hope they'll be very happy. Clare is very maternal. It wouldn't be impossible for her to have a couple of babies, or they could adopt. As for me, I'm planning to expand the agency. I think I might take Carl on. Advertising and PR are close relations and I've known and liked him a long time, on a purely platonic basis.'

'He was married once, wasn't he?'

'A long time ago. One of those very young marriages which so often don't work out because the people involved haven't found out who they are, let alone the sort of partner they need.'

'Mm, if Tom had persuaded me to marry him before I had spread my wings, I think we'd have split up. There's a lot to be said for staying single until you're our age. Although I confess there were nights, before Tom came back into my life, when I lay awake wondering if I would ever find the man for me.'

As if realising this might be a tactless thing to say to someone who was still on her own, Sasha added, rather too quickly, 'But I was much happier single than a lot of women are married.'

'And the great thing about your career is that you can take it with you, selling Australian features to your markets here and working up new markets there. I couldn't transplant myself nearly so easily,' said Rosie.

The following morning they parted with hugs and kisses and bright smiles. But that night, the knowledge that Sasha was not away for a few days but had gone for good and by now was well on the way to the other side of the world where, if all went well with them, she was likely to remain for the rest of her life, made Rosie feel deeply depressed.

She went to bed early and, when she had put out the light, curled up on her side and, as she had ten years ago on the night of the farewell party when Nick left his job on the *News*, wept, both for the loss of her friend as well as the collapse of her hope that, this time, her love for Nick would not end in heartbreak.

The first desolate days after Sasha's departure stretched into weeks and then months and the intervals between her letters describing life in Australia gradually grew longer.

Rosie had wondered if, after the novelty of life Down Under had worn off, her friend might begin to feel homesick. But as, in England, the long summer evenings began to shorten, Sasha's enthusiasm for her new environment, where the weather was hotting up, showed no sign of diminishing.

She loved the better climate, the beauty of the Blue Mountains where she and Tom spent their weekends, the view of Sydney harbour from their top-floor apartment, their mainly outdoor social life of barbecues and parties on boats, in fact every aspect of life in a country which she now considered 'makes Europe seem tired and grey by comparison'.

Clare, after reading this comment at the end of Sasha's latest letter which Rosie had passed across the breakfast table on a morning when the drizzle descending from a sky the colour of grey flannel looked likely to continue all day, said, 'It's nice that she's settled down so well. I shouldn't want to move so far away myself, but on a day like this one can't help envying Nick. He's probably floating in his swimming pool under a sky as blue as his marvellous eyes.'

Having said this, she jumped up and began to clear the table, clearly embarrassed by her unguarded remark. It confirmed Rosie's intuition that Nick was often in her housekeeper's thoughts.

She herself tried never to think of him except when she was forced to do so by matters to do with *Crusade*.

So far he had not made use of the now empty flat at the top of the house. She had been told by Anna, who had heard it from Carolyn, that he was working flat-out on his second book which he wanted to finish before the first one was published and he was involved in its promotion. After that, according to Anna, he was planning to take off for six months. It seemed there were parts of the world his job had not taken him to which he wanted to see.

Rosie did not go to Spain for the sales conference which Bury & Poole held there that autumn. But she was told about it by Anna, who said that Nick's talk to the reps had been one of the most brilliant author's talks she had ever heard.

Apparently from the pay-off line of his opening anecdote he had kept them in stitches.

'Clean funny stories, what's more,' said Anna. 'Nothing even vaguely smutty. All true behind-the-scenes stories from his time in TV. He'll have them falling off their chairs at the Foyle's and *Yorkshire Post* luncheons. Taking him round the country is going to be a piece of cake for you.'

'It looks like it, yes,' said Rosie, inwardly dreading it.

*   *   *

The first time Nick used the flat, he rang Clare a few days beforehand so that Rosie had time to cook up a reason to be out of town while he was in London. She felt that he would be pleased to find her away, and although she would have to face him eventually she wanted to postpone that uncomfortable moment as long as possible.

On the morning of his arrival and her departure for Yorkshire, she was packing her suitcase when she heard singing in the room overhead.

Clare had already spent a day spring-cleaning the flat and now she was upstairs making up the bed. It was obvious that she was delighted Nick was coming to stay. At first Rosie thought she had the radio with her. Then she realised it was Clare who was singing. It must be a spontaneous expression of her eagerness to see his 'marvellous blue eyes' again.

In Yorkshire, with north-country bluntness, almost everyone she met told her she was looking peaky.

'You haven't gone and got that disease, have you?' her mother asked anxiously, when Rosie was unable to finish a huge helping of apple pudding and whipped cream.

'Anorexia? No, of course not, Mum. Look what I had for breakfast: two eggs, bacon, a sausage, a fried tomato and a fried potato.'

'But you didn't have any cereal or toast and marmalade and you've been out in the fresh air all morning.'

Her family's concern about what they considered her thinness and lack of appetite made it a relief to return to her own home.

Clare, to whom she had spoken before setting out, wanting to be sure that Nick had left according to plan, was out when she arrived. But there was a note on the table by the door saying that she would be back in time to get Rosie's supper.

The living-room was full of flowers which had not been there when Rosie left. There was also a new hardback novel by Clare's favourite author on the coffee-table. Rosie opened it at the fly-leaf, but although it was obviously a present from Nick he had not inscribed it.

She had unpacked and changed her clothes but was still in her bedroom when she heard the front door being unlocked. A few moments later Clare came running up the stairs.

When she appeared in the doorway, her eyes had a sparkle Rosie had never seen in them before. Instead of asking about Rosie's visit and the drive back, which was how she usually greeted her after an absence, she said eagerly, 'I'm so glad you're back. I've got something to tell you.'

CHAPTER TWELVE

'IT'S ALL rather complicated,' said Clare, 'And I'll tell you the whole story later. The important thing is——' she paused, her eyes filling with tears even though she was smiling '—I'm going to be married.'

The hardest thing Rosie had ever had to do was to jump up and put her arms round her and say, while her heart was breaking, 'That's wonderful news, Clare. You deserve to be happy.'

'You don't seem at all surprised,' Clare said, when they drew apart.

'Hardly. I've seen it coming. The only surprise is that Nick has gone back to Spain.'

'Nick?' said Clare, looking puzzled. 'Why shouldn't he go back?'

'I'd have thought he wouldn't want to let you out of his sight . . . or vice versa.'

'You didn't think I was talking about Nick, did you?' Clare exclaimed.

With a catch in her throat, Rosie said, 'Weren't you?'

'Of course not, you silly girl. You're the one Nick is in love with. I'm going to marry Robert.'

'Robert?' Rosie said faintly.

'Robert Southwold . . . Angie's father.'

'Oh . . . oh, well, that's wonderful.' Rosie sat down on her bed, feeling strangely weak at the knees, which she had always thought a mere figure of speech and now found was not. 'What in the world makes you think Nick is in love with me?'

'His visible disappointment on finding that you'd gone away and wouldn't be back until after he'd left. The way he questioned me about you. The fact that he looks as fed up as you have lately.'

'That's all supposition,' said Rosie.

'Am I wrong in thinking that you love him?'

Rosie bent her head while trying to swallow the lump in her throat. Suddenly her emotions were too strong to be contained. She bowed her back, buried her face in her hands and burst into tears.

Clare came and sat beside her and put a comforting arm round her heaving shoulders.

Presently, when the tears were abating, she said gently, 'I knew I was right. You do love him . . . and I'm certain he feels the same way about you. I'll get the tissues——' this as Rosie began to wipe her eyes with her fingers.

'I—I'm sorry to carry on like this. It's just the relief of finding that it's not Nick you're going to marry. But let's not talk about him. I want to hear all about Robert. When am I going to meet him? Does Angie know he's her father? Has she always known?'

Clare shook her head. 'She thought her father was dead, but I'll explain all that later. What *I* want to know is, what has gone wrong between you and Nick? Something has, obviously. Are you sure it can't be put right?'

So then Rosie told her the whole story, starting with falling in love with him when she was seventeen and ending with Carl coming down the stairs and Nick stalking out of the house.

'If he loves you, naturally he would be upset at thinking you were on intimate terms with another man, which is how it must have appeared to him,' said Clare. 'In your place I'd have written him a note telling him he had jumped to a false conclusion.'

'Would you?' Rosie said doubtfully. 'I was angry with him for interpreting the facts in the nastiest possible way and for taking such a sexist attitude. He claims that he isn't and never has been a womaniser, and that may be true. But how many men who at the age of thirty-five are still unmarried haven't had several close relationships with women? None, I should imagine. What right had Nick to expect me to have lived like a nun until he appeared?'

'I'm sure he didn't expect that. What riled him, I should imagine, was thinking that you were *still* involved with someone else. If, that night, he was on the point of telling you how he felt about you, Carl's appearing like that must have been a bad shock to him.'

'But if Carl and I had been having an affair, Carl wouldn't have made that remark about Sasha and I pampering ourselves. He'd have known we had a jacuzzi. What he said was conclusive evidence that I wasn't involved with him.'

'Strong evidence, not conclusive. Anyway Nick may not have taken it in. He knows now that you didn't go on a cycling holiday last summer and that, to the best of my knowledge, you haven't had a date with Carl or anyone else for months.'

'You didn't *tell* him you thought I was in love with him, did you?' Rosie demanded, in a fit of panic.

'If I had, you'd have had him on your parents' doorstep, demanding to see you. I'm sure of that. No,

I only said that you worked too hard and could do with a relaxing holiday. I hoped it might enter his head to set up a Christmas house party and invite you to join it. Let's go down and have a cup of tea.'

Before going downstairs, Rosie cleaned off her smeared eye make-up and washed her tear-streaked face.

She was ashamed of herself for crying in front of Clare. It had been reaction to the awful shock of believing, for a few unforgettably anguished minutes, that very soon she would have to attend the wedding of the only man she had ever truly loved, or would ever love, to another woman.

'Now I insist on hearing all about Robert,' she said, when she joined Clare in the kitchen.

'There's not a great deal to tell. As soon as he walked on to the conductor's rostrum at the Barbican, I knew my feelings hadn't changed since I last saw him twenty years ago. I'd seen photographs of him, of course. But it's not the same as seeing someone in the flesh. Then, not long after that concert, Angie said he wanted to meet me to talk about her future. How was I to say no? But I didn't want her to be present at our first meeting so I rang him up and suggested he call at a time when she would be safely out of the way.'

'Did he recognise you?' Rosie asked.

'Instantly. He had begun to suspect that he would. You see, the first time he met Angie she reminded him of someone but he couldn't think who. Then one day his mother mentioned her eldest sister who had died of pneumonia when she was only twenty-three. Robert had seen a studio portrait of his aunt but not for a long time. He asked his mother to find the album it was in and, when he saw it again, his aunt's likeness to Angie was as strong as if they were twins.'

Clare paused to pour out some more tea before she continued, 'His first thought was not that he was Angie's father but that his grandfather had sown some wild oats and she must be descended from one of the old man's by-blows. But a distant relationship didn't seem to explain why he liked Angie so much more than any of the other young people chosen for his special classes on musicianship. When he questioned her about her family, she told him what I had told her: that her father and I were planning to marry but that he had been killed. She grew up thinking his name was James Curtis, a name I invented.'

'Why?'

'Because at the time I thought it would complicate her life to know that she was the daughter of someone I always felt would become famous—as Robert has. Children who, for any reason, have never known one of their parents are always curious about them. I considered it best for everyone to keep her father's real identity a secret. He hadn't known I was pregnant when we said goodbye to each other.'

'Why did you say goodbye?'

'Because Robert was going to America to continue his studies there. We had been students together but by then I knew my voice fell short of being first class. I had been in love with him for months but his feelings weren't as deep. He was obsessed with music. He only made love to me once, after a student party at which we had both drunk enough to impair our judgement. I knew he didn't want to marry me so, although I had missed a period, I said nothing. But this was over twenty years ago and I'd had an old-fashioned upbringing. I felt it was my punishment for doing what I had been taught to believe was wrong.'

'Oh, Clare...how unhappy and frightened you must have been.'

'Yes, especially when my stepfather called me a slut and sent me packing. Never mind: that was long ago and it's turned out all right in the end. You see when we met again Robert had begun to realise what he was missing. He was ready for marriage.'

'How did Angie react when you told her the truth?'

'Amazingly well. I was afraid she would be angry with me for deceiving her, even though with good intentions.'

'But she wasn't?'

'She understood why I'd done it. She said that, if she had known whose child she really was, it would have been unbearable not being able to claim the relationship if he had been married with other children born in wedlock. Or if he had rejected her. As things stand, she's overjoyed at finding out she is his daughter and he wants everyone to know it.'

'Will you mind that?'

'Why should I? I have never concealed the fact that I'm an unmarried mother...although not for much longer.'

'How soon am I going to lose you?'

'Not yet...not until you've found a replacement. I wouldn't leave you in the lurch and nor can Robert leave his mother. She needs him. His father's long illness is an appalling strain on her. So we're going to get married very quietly but we shan't set up home together while his father's alive. After he dies, we'll take his mother to live in Switzerland with us. She's

a nice old lady. I shall be glad to look after her for
whatever few years remain to her, pool old soul.'

Nick did not fulfil Clare's hope that he would include
Rosie in a Christmas house party at the monastery.

This year, unable to face being force-fed in
Yorkshire, she splurged a great deal of money on
flying by Concorde to Australia to spend a fortnight
with Sasha and Tom.

The change of scene, the warm weather and having
nothing to do did her good. She did not pour out her
heart to Sasha as she had to Clare.

Sasha was excited because she had decided to have
a baby. Rosie didn't want to cloud her friend's happiness by admitting her own wretchedness, nor did
she want to discuss the fact that Nick had declined
an invitation to Clare's small, very private wedding.

If Clare's theory that he loved Rosie was correct,
why hadn't he seized that opportunity to make contact
with her?

The publication of *Crusade* was now only weeks
ahead. As she flew back to Europe in the luxury which
had taken such a large slice out of her bank balance,
she reflected that the next time she travelled by air
was likely to be with Nick, en route to Glasgow on
the first leg of the extensive author tour she had
planned for him, every detail mapped out on a twenty-
page tour schedule which, as well as being stored in
the memory of the office computer, was fixed in her
own memory.

She could see it in her mind's eye.

Author Tour Schedule: *Crusade*—Nicholas
Winchester.

As of 23 December

Day One: Monday 4 February

9.15 a.m.: Shuttle departs Heathrow (check-in time 20 minutes absolute minimum)

10.25 a.m.: Shuttle arrives Glasgow

11.30 a.m.: *Daily Record* Interview with (journalist to be confirmed) *Circulation: 765,000 Venue: the Albany Hotel

And so on for page after page of carefully timed and meticulously planned appointments which should bring Nick and his book to the notice of as many newspaper readers, radio listeners and TV viewers as possible and give Bury & Poole maximum value for the high cost of the week's tour.

She wondered how he would stand up to it. Pretty well, probably. She expected to end it exhausted. Not because she would be responsible for dealing with any hitches which cropped up. She could cope with that. It was the strain of being with him which would leave her drained.

She both longed for and dreaded meeting him.

On Monday February the fourth, Rosie climbed out of the chauffeur-driven car which would shortly be taking her and Nick to Heathrow but which at the moment was parked outside the Arlington Street entrance to the Ritz Hotel.

Bury & Poole were paying for him to stay there throughout the tour except on Wednesday night when he, and she, would be staying at a country house hotel in Lancashire where he had a full day of interviews in Manchester followed by another in Liverpool.

'Would you tell Mr Winchester that Miss Middleton is here with the car to take him to the airport, please?' she said to the porter on duty at the reception desk.

In spite of the hotel's reputation for impeccable service, on her way home last night she had checked that everything was in order in his white and gold suite overlooking Green Park. Anna had intended meeting him at the airport but he had told her not to bother. He would see her at the dinner party being given for him by the managing director of Bury & Poole and his wife in their luxurious penthouse on the top floor of the firm's offices which since early Victorian days had been housed in a historic building in Piccadilly.

Rosie had given a great deal of thought to what to wear for this first day with Nick. As she waited for him to appear, she knew that she looked both chic and businesslike in her expensive raincoat and comfortable but smart black patent leather boots with low heels. Under the coat was an uncrushable dress, bought on her trip to New York, ideal for days like the one ahead of her.

She expected Nick to emerge from the lift or come down stairs near the desk. But her first sight of him was at the far end of the wide corridor which stretched from this end of the hotel to the glass doors of the famous dining-room at the other end.

The sight of him striding towards her along the hundred-yard expanse of deep carpet made her heart turn cartwheels. She had a crazy impulse to start running to meet him, her arms wide, her face alight with the joy that seeing him gave her.

But instead she remained where she was, outwardly composed, until he was near enough for her to smile and say, 'Good morning. I hope they didn't keep you up too late last night. Have you had breakfast?'

'Good morning.' Nick returned her smile as he took her outstretched hand in the strong, warm clasp which always sent a sensuous shiver down her spine. 'I was in bed by midnight and yes, I have had breakfast, thank you. How are you, Rosie?'

'Very well, thank you. And you?' she enquired politely.

'I'm well but——' his dark brows contracted '—I know you'll be sorry to hear that Marie-Laure died last month.'

'Oh, Nick—no! Oh, that *is* sad news.' With an involuntary gesture of sympathy she put her hand over his left hand which he was holding in front of him because he was carrying a raincoat over his arm.

'It's the reason I haven't been over here before now. Unfortunately she wasn't granted her wish for a quick, easy end. I couldn't leave her. Spanish hospitals rely on the patients' families and friends to give them a lot of the attention they would receive from the staff in hospitals in other countries. A lot of people enjoyed her lunch parties and her amusing stories, but not so many wanted to keep her company when she was seriously ill.'

'Why didn't you let me know? I would have come to Spain instead of going to Australia.'

'She didn't want you to know or to see her laid low.'

The driver came through the revolving door. 'If you want to be sure of catching the nine-fifteen shuttle, we'd best be on our way, miss.'

'Yes, thank you, we're coming.'

The news of the Frenchwoman's death made Rosie forget the list of impersonal topics she had had in mind to avoid an uncomfortable silence on the way to the airport.

They were passing the Victoria & Albert Museum when she said, 'Was that why you didn't come to Clare's wedding?'

He nodded. 'She knew the reason but I made her promise not to tell you.'

'It must have been a very sad Christmas for you,' she said quietly. 'You were such close friends in spite of the age gap.'

'I shall miss her,' he agreed, his eyes sombre. 'Having no near relations, she has left her house to me, but she wanted you to have some of the things in it.'

'Me? But she scarcely knew me. We only met twice.'

'She liked you on sight. After meeting you the first time she said you were a rare combination of intelligence, beauty and character. I agreed with her.'

Rosie flashed an uncertain glance at him through her lashes. 'And then revised your opinion the next night,' she said.

'I forgot the rule drummed into me years ago when I was a cub reporter. "Check your facts". I know now I was mistaken in the inference I drew. I apologise for that false conclusion.'

'I have an apology of mine own to make,' she said. 'I lied to you about the bicycle tour. I don't make a habit of being untruthful.'

'According to Clare, who must know you as well as anyone, you're a paragon of all the virtues.'

'She exaggerates.'

'On the contrary, she is one of the most sensible, level-headed women I've met, with excellent judgement.' After a slight pause, he added, 'She's had a difficult life and made the best of it. Even now she won't find it easy being married to a man as dedicated to his art as Southwold, but she sounds very happy.'

'She *glows* with happiness. When the tour is over, she wants you to meet Robert and the four of us must discuss what is to be done about the house.'

'There are many things to discuss,' he said, 'but this isn't the time or the place. I see from the schedule that I'm even tied up in the evenings.'

'You'll enjoy having dinner with *Sunday Post*'s woman's page editor. She's an intelligent, interesting woman who, as you're an ex-journalist, will probably tell you some of her very funny stories about famous people she's met.'

'And what are you going to be doing while I'm dining with her?'

'I'm going to be entertaining a couple of useful contacts. When I took over the agency, the woman who founded it warned me never to lose touch with the network of contacts she had built up in the provinces. It's fatally easy for people who work in London to think it's the centre of the universe. It isn't. Everywhere is the centre of the universe to the people who live there.'

The special departure lounge for shuttle passengers was full of dark-suited businessmen with expensive attaché- and briefcases. Boarding took place on time but then the shuttle was held up in a queue of aircraft waiting to take off. Even inside the cabin of the flight to Scotland they could feel the thunderous reverberation as a Concorde took off.

This led Nick to ask about her trip to Australia and they talked about Oz, as he called it, all the way to Glasgow.

The taxi drive from the airport to the Albany Hotel was their last time alone that day. Sitting in on his first interview with a columnist from the *Daily Record* confirmed Rosie's belief that it was going to be the most successful tour she had ever organised. Not because of her expertise but because of his.

The next day, in Edinburgh, went off without any hitches. She had warned Nick that there was considerable rivalry between the two cities and that he should watch out for questions designed to elicit unguarded 'quotes' about which of the two he preferred.

On Wednesday they flew to Manchester for a third day of non-stop interviews, the last being on evening TV. When this was over a car was waiting to take them to the expensive hotel where, for the first time, they would be at leisure until bedtime.

Stretching out his long legs in the back of the spacious limousine sent by the car-hire company, Nick said, 'I have to compliment you on your masterly planning, Rosie. But, even with you in charge, anyone who takes part in this circus on a regular basis has to be crazy. By the end of Day One I was sick of the sound of my own voice and wishing I'd dug my heels in when Anna mooted this tour. There is only one compensation.'

'What's that?'

'I'll tell you later. Right now, if you'll excuse me, I'm going to take a catnap.'

As he arranged his tall frame in a comfortable position, she remembered him saying, in Spain, that the knack of taking short naps was one he had learned on his foreign assignments.

Already, within moments of closing his eyes, his body was at ease, his conscious mind switched off. He looked as if the only unrelaxed muscles in his body were the ones which kept his jaw from dropping and his mouth closed.

Repose ironed out the laughter-lines and the deep grooves carved in his cheeks. He looked younger, traces of boyishness still to be seen in the good-looking face which, alert, was that of a rather cynical, worldly wise man who had seen many terrible things and been in some tough spots.

A wave of love and tenderness for him swept over her. Feasting her eyes on him in a way that was impossible when he was awake, she understood for the first time that, inside the self-possessed man who could so easily puncture her own self-possession, there was another very private person. A man with many friends but no family behind him, a man who had recently supported someone he cared for through a fatal illness, a man who, like all human beings, needed to come first in someone's heart.

She longed to take him in her arms and cradle his head against her shoulder.

As the car left the city behind and the moon rose over a landscape still unexpectedly rural in a region associated with 'dark Satanic mills', Rosie made up her mind that, before this night was out, she would hold Nick in her arms.

CHAPTER THIRTEEN

A LOG fire was blazing in the hall of the hotel when they arrived. There was a lavish arrangement of hothouse flowers on the desk where they both signed the register.

Normally, when taking a man on tour, Rosie asked for rooms on different floors. This time she had left it to chance. They might have been given rooms next door to each other or at opposite ends of the building.

They were escorted upstairs by the manager. He had seen Nick on TV in the past and also the regional news programme he had just appeared on.

Rosie's room was near the lift, overlooking the entrance to the substantial mansion built, according to the brochure, by a rich Victorian mill owner.

Her luggage had already been brought up and the porter had turned on all the lights in a luxurious bedroom furnished with twin brass beds and massive mahogany wardrobe in keeping with the age of the house. A great deal of money had been spent combining the solid comfort of a past age with the conveniences of present day, and she knew the hotel drew its patrons from as far afield as America.

'This is one of our nicest rooms. I hope you'll be comfortable, Miss Middleton,' said the manager.

'I'm sure I shall, thank you.'

As he turned to escort Nick to his room, Nick said, 'I'm going to take a shower, Rosie. See you later.'

'OK.' She gave a smile and a tip to the baggage porter and closed the door of her room.

Now, at last, they would be alone together and undisturbed until the car came to take them to Liverpool for more interviews before they returned to London for a major chat-show appearance followed by the launch party in a private room at the Ritz tomorrow night. On Friday there was a signing session at Hatchards, followed by Saturday in Bristol, Sunday free, and then three more days of visiting provincial cities.

But for the next twelve hours they were on their own, on what amounted to their first ever date, an occasion she had first dreamed of ten years ago. Ten minutes later her case was unpacked. Twenty minutes later she had taken off her make-up, had a refreshing hot shower and rinsed out her bra, briefs and tights. By the time she had been in her room half an hour, she was wearing new Italian undies, and a new dovegrey silk robe bought especially for the tour, and was putting the finishing touches to her evening make-up.

With that done, she planned to fix herself a gin and tonic and sip it slowly until Nick called her on the internal telephone to fix a time to meet for dinner.

It was only then that she discovered her room did not have an honour bar. Drinks had to be ordered from room service.

As well as the door to her bathroom, the bedroom had another door connecting it with the next room but at present locked or perhaps permanently closed and sound-proofed.

The sound-proofing wasn't perfect. She could hear the muffled murmur of men's voices and other sounds suggesting that her neighbours were having a meal served upstairs.

The line to room service was engaged and it was a time of night when the staff were likely to be fully extended. But as always Rosie had what she called her St Bernard supply of liquor.

She had blotted her lipstick and sprayed on her favourite scent, and was opening the drawer where she had stowed a half-bottle of gin, when there was a tap at the door.

Thinking it might be the housekeeper coming to see if she had everything she wanted, she called, 'Come in.'

But instead of hearing a pass-key in the lock of the door to the landing, she was amazed to see, in the largest of the triple mirrors, the connecting door open and Nick standing behind her, wearing a dark silk dressing-gown.

'You must be ready for a revitalising shot of something, aren't you?' he said, as she stared at his reflection in surprise. 'I have some champagne on ice if that appeals to you? Or would you rather have a Martini or a G and T?'

'Champagne sounds wonderful.' She rose from the dressing-stool. 'Is that your bedroom?'

'No, it's our sitting-room. I thought, as the dining-room here is open to non-residents and is usually full, it would be more relaxing to have dinner here by ourselves.'

'But I didn't reserve a suite.'

'I did. You aren't the only one who has contacts. I know a guy on the editorial staff of the *Liverpool Echo*. He brings his wife here for their anniversaries. He fixed it for me.'

'I see,' said Rosie. 'Well, I'm not quite dressed yet. I'll join you in a minute.'

'Why not stay in that pretty dressing-gown? I'm planning to dine in mine...if you have no objection?' He lifted an eyebrow but otherwise his expression was enigmatic.

As she stood up she saw that although her legs were bare and her feet thrust into matching quilted silk travel-mules, he was wearing trousers under the dressing-gown, with loafers but no socks.

'Why not?' she said.

A log fire, sufficiently deceptive to pass at first glance for a real one, was burning in the adjoining sitting-room. A table spread with a long pale pink damask cloth was set for *diner à deux* near two tall velvet-curtained windows. A comfortable sofa was placed facing the fire with armchairs on either side. A large low glass-topped coffee-table served all three.

'This is much more peaceful than a public dining-room,' she said, sitting down on the sofa while Nick went to open the bottle in a bucket on a side-table. 'Was your nap in the car enough to revive you after the rigours of three days on the road?'

'The sight of you in that outfit would revive any man,' he said. 'To rephrase the old song...firelight becomes you. I noticed that in the library at my house.' He brought her a glass of pink champagne and, with another in his free hand, sat down beside her.

'What shall we drink to?' he asked.

'To your book, of course.' She raised her glass. 'To *Crusade*...here's hoping it stays at number one for many, many weeks and puts you among the top names in popular fiction. I'm quite sure it will.'

'Thank you. I'll drink to that.' But it was a sip taken in acknowledgement of the toast she had proposed rather than with a hearty swig that Nick sampled the champagne. 'Do you remember the Spanish toast we drank to at my house?' he asked.

'I've forgotten the Spanish but the translation was "Health and money and the time to enjoy them", wasn't it?'

'That's right. I'd like to drink to an adaptation of that. Health and money and someone to share them with.'

The way he was looking at her, his blue eyes as brilliant as jewels in his bronzed face, the deep tan all the more striking in this climate at this season, made Rosie catch her breath.

Her voice was slightly unsteady as she repeated his version of the old toast.

And then, as she was about to drink to it, Nick touched the rim of his glass to the rim of hers and said, 'That someone being you, my love. Will you marry me, Rosie?'

For a moment she could not answer, too overjoyed to speak. Because, although every instinct had told her that tonight she would sleep in his arms, she had not been sure that he would first say, 'I love you', and she certainly hadn't expected an old-fashioned, formal proposal.

When she could find her voice, and the words to express what she felt, she said huskily, 'I will marry you, and love you, and care for you all my life.'

And then, at the same moment, they both put their glasses aside and Nick took her in his arms, at first gently and then, unable to leash any longer the force of his feelings, crushing her against his chest in a fiercely possessive hug before kissing her in a manner which would have shocked the mill owner's unmarried daughters but to which Rosie responded with a pent-up ardour to match his.

But very soon kisses were not enough to express the depth of their need and longing for each other. Leaving the ice-cold champagne to grow tepid in the heat from the fire, Nick scooped her up with the same easy strength she had first experienced in the garden at Font Vella and carried her into his bedroom.

They were married in the village church where Rosie had been christened and confirmed and been a bridesmaid to her sisters.

Unlike their weddings, hers was a quiet affair held by special licence and attended only by her parents, sisters and brothers-in-law and Nick's closest friend and best man, the TV cameraman who had been in numerous perilous situations with him.

Rosie wore a simple dress of ivory georgette with a small Thirties-style hat with a fine silk veil. She carried a bouquet of mimosa brought by a courier service from the monastery garden where Nick had planted the seven different kinds of mimosa which grew in Spain.

After an informal wedding breakfast prepared by Mrs Middleton, Rosie changed into travelling clothes and left the bouquet in a vase to bring a touch of spring to her parents' sitting-room.

She and Nick had discussed various exotic locations for their honeymoon but they all involved long flights and in the end Rosie had said, 'We have all our lives to travel together. I can't think of anywhere nicer to start our marriage than El Monasterio...unless that would be dull for you?'

'Well, yes, it will be rather dull with nothing to do but make love to you, but as it's only for two weeks I guess I can stand it.'

It was dark when they arrived at Font Vella. Rosie was reminded of the night she had come to the village with Anna and Carolyn, dreading the confrontation with the man who was now her husband. Tonight she jumped out of the taxi eagerly, her heart full of joyous anticipation as she looked up at the wonderful display of stars which, if the sky had been equally clear and bright last time, she had been too preoccupied to notice.

Encarna was waiting to greet them. She had unlocked and opened the huge heavy doors with their pattern of metal bosses. As the taxi driver dealt with the luggage, Nick swept Rosie off her feet and carried her across the threshold of their home.

Encarna did not stay long. Very soon the great doors were closed and bolted once more and they were alone.

They had not dined on the plane, knowing a better meal would be awaiting them. They ate by the fire in the library, at the same time reading the congratulatory messages and other matter which Nick's fax machine had cut and collated in his absence.

The machine was going to make it possible for Rosie to continue to run the agency from Spain. For the time being she would have to spend one week in four in London, but sometimes Nick would come with her. Although part of her longed to settle down and devote herself to her husband and their children like her mother and sisters, she knew that to be completely fulfilled she needed the stimulus of her work.

Nick gave a low whistle. 'Look at this!'

He passed her a letter from Carolyn, informing him that an American book club had made a stupendous offer for *Crusade*. Earlier they had seen the book on sale at Gatwick airport and Carolyn also mentioned that the first printing had sold so well that a second edition was being printed.

'Darling, that's wonderful. What have I done to deserve a husband who is kind, clever, handsome and on the way to becoming a millionaire?'

He grinned. 'You're prejudiced. Also this run of luck may not last. My next book may be a flop. It happens. Anyway, as far as I'm concerned, fame and fortune are fine but they're nothing compared to having you on the other side of the table for the rest of my life.'

'That's exactly how I feel,' she told him softly.

HARLEQUIN
Romance®

**HARLEQUIN ROMANCE
IS BETTING ON LOVE!**

And The Bridal Collection's
September title is a sure bet.

JACK OF HEARTS (#3218)
by Heather Allison

THE BRIDAL COLLECTION

THE BRIDE played her part.
THE GROOM played for keeps.
THEIR WEDDING was in the cards!

Available in August in
THE BRIDAL COLLECTION:

THE BEST-MADE PLANS (#3214)
by Leigh Michaels

Harlequin Romance

Wherever Harlequin
books are sold.